W9-CAW-820

Cousins in the Castle

Books by Barbara Brooks Wallace

Peppermints in the Parlor

The Barrel in the Basement

Perfect Acres, Inc.

The Twin in the Tavern

Cousins in the Castle

Cousins in the Castle

Barbara Brooks Wallace

[MYSTERY]

FIC
WALLACE

A Jean Karl Book

Atheneum Books for Young Readers

MANHASSET PUBLIC LIBRARY

Atheneum Books for Young Readers
An imprint of Simon & Schuster Children's Publishing Division
1230 Avenue of the Americas
New York, New York 10020

Copyright © 1996 by Barbara Brooks Wallace
All rights reserved including the right of reproduction in whole or in part in any form.
Book design by Virginia Pope
The text of this book is set in Bembo.

First Edition
Printed in the United States of America
10 9 8 7 6 5 4 3 2

Library of Congress Cataloging-in-Publication Data
Wallace, Barbara Brooks.
Cousins in the castle / Barbara Brooks Wallace. — 1st ed.
p. cm.
"A Jean Karl book."
Summary: A new friend comes to Amelia's rescue
when she finds herself the victim of a dastardly villain's fiendish plans.
ISBN 0-689-80637-X
[1. Adventure and adventurers—Fiction. 2. Friendship—Fiction.]
I. Title
PZ7.W1547Cr 1996
[Fic]—dc20
95-23484

For my very own granddaughter, Elizabeth Noel,
her very own book, with love
—B. B. W.

Contents

Chapter 1

Cousin Charlotte

Four months!

How, Amelia wondered, could four months have had such a wonderful beginning and then such a grim and terrible ending? How could four months have made such a change in her life that even the streets now looked different to her? *Then*, the gaslights had winked at her cheerfully, and people strolling down the streets somehow all looked as if they might be going to a party or a dance. Now the very same lights stared through the deepening fog of late afternoon with unblinking, indifferent eyes. The people trudged along with leaden steps, looking like nothing more than faceless shadows returning to their dark, dreary homes.

Four months! Four months! It almost seemed as if the horses' hooves clop-clopping dismally on the damp streets were mocking her with the words. With her black, high-button shoes neatly crossed, her hands folded tightly in her lap, she looked out the cab window and tried desperately not to let the tears spill down her cheeks. Although who was there to care whether or not she was crying? Certainly not the stone-faced woman sitting off in the opposite corner of the cab as far from Amelia as she could get. It was as if she could not bear the thought of even touching anything so distasteful as a child, much less comforting one in her arms.

Four months! Could it be only four months since the memorable evening when Amelia had been escorted by Papa to dine at Belding House, one of the most elegant hotels in all of London? Barely turned eleven, how grown-up she had felt that evening! She was not only to be permitted to stay up well past her bedtime, but in addition, her beloved nursemaid, Polly, had insisted that she also be permitted to wear her straight brown hair piled stylishly on top of her head. Ordinarily, of course, she was obliged to wear it in braids each day to Mrs. Draper's Select Academy for Girls, the school she attended.

"My, but you look the young lady, Miss Amelia Fairwick!" Polly had exclaimed.

And Amelia felt that she did, too, with her hair piled up and her new rose velveteen dress with the wide lace collar bought for the occasion. And how her locket of pure gold glistened against the velveteen! It was her most treasured possession, having once belonged to beautiful Mama, who was carried off by fever when Amelia was but two weeks old. It was Mama's photograph that was in the locket.

But on that special night, they were to celebrate the birthday of another person who had become very special to Amelia—Aunt Felicia. She was not Amelia's aunt, it must be explained, but Felicia Charlton, the widow of a dear friend of Papa's. Aunt Felicia had herself become very dear to him, so dear, in truth, that on that night they announced to Amelia that Aunt Felicia was soon to become Felicia Fairwick!

Not long after that announcement, however, Papa had to make a business trip, which had been planned for some time, to his company's overseas business connection in the Near East. He would not be away for long, he said, but long enough that Amelia would have to enter Mrs. Draper's Academy as a boarding student while he was away. Still, Aunt Felicia would visit her often, and

Papa promised he would write every day, a promise he kept faithfully. Then, quite suddenly, the letters stopped coming—to Amelia, to Aunt Felicia, and even to Papa's place of business.

But one terrible, never-to-be-forgotten day, a letter did come, except that it was not from Papa. It was from a man in his overseas office. There had been a deadly fire at Mr. Fairwick's hotel, said the letter, and he was lost with many others. Mr. Fairwick was no more!

"Oh, Aunt Felicia!" Amelia sobbed, for it was Felicia Charlton who had been the bearer of the dread tidings. "Papa is gone forever!"

"Forever!" whispered Aunt Felicia, as if she needed to echo that word in order to believe it.

"And I have not only lost Papa," Amelia cried, "but now there will never be a wedding. You will never be my new mama!"

"Perhaps not by law," replied Aunt Felicia. "But remember this, you will always be my darling child, no matter what."

No matter what! The words sounded ominous, but Amelia chose to give all her attention to the words that had come just before them. "If . . . if I am always to be your child, does that mean I will come to live with you?" she asked. "Isn't that what Papa would have wished?"

"Oh yes!" Aunt Felicia said fervently. "But we will have to wait and see."

Wait and see! Wait and see *what*? Ominous words again. But Aunt Felicia did not go on to explain them. And it was not until late the following day before Amelia would learn their meaning. She was to have a guardian, who must be her nearest blood relative. That turned out to be a cousin of Mama's—Cousin Basil—and Amelia would have to go and live with him.

"But. . . but I don't know of any Cousin Basil!" cried Amelia to Aunt Felicia. "I don't remember Papa ever speaking of him."

"He may have many years ago, dear child, but has had no reason to do so in more recent years," said Aunt Felicia. "Cousin Basil is, after all, only a distant cousin, I believe. But there is indeed such a person."

"C . . . couldn't Mr. Collingwood arrange for you to be my guardian instead?" Amelia pleaded, for she had often heard Papa say laughingly that Mr. Collingwood, his solicitor, could arrange almost anything.

But Aunt Felicia shook her head. "I'm afraid that only your Cousin Basil can now decide that, and we must not hang on to any false hopes about it."

"Still, even if you are not my guardian, Aunt Felicia, you can come to visit me all the time," Amelia said eagerly. "You . . . you will do that, won't you?"

"Oh, if only that were possible," replied Aunt Felicia. "But it appears that your cousin is not only distant on your family tree, but also distant in that he lives far from here. So very, very far."

Amelia's throat grew tight. "Wh . . . where?" she asked.

Aunt Felicia hesitated. "In . . . in America."

"America!" Amelia breathed in horror. She could have been no more stricken had she been told she was to journey to the moon.

"Yes, right in New York, where you were born, darling child." Aunt Felicia forced a dim smile. "So you see, Amelia, you are really going home!"

Home, indeed! Amelia had been brought to London when she was a baby, so how could she think of anyplace else as home? Oh, she knew Papa had said that one day they might return to America, but the words "one day" had had no more reality than the words "once upon a time" in a fairy tale. And at the moment, her home was surely where she was right then. But what could a child of eleven do about it? Nothing, it appeared.

For awhile, Amelia cherished the fond hope that Cousin Basil would inform Mr. Collingwood that he no more wanted her as a charge than she wanted him for a guardian. But that hope vanished forever when, shortly after, she learned that someone would soon be on the way by ship to fetch her. As it was considered improper for a gentleman to accompany a young girl on such a long journey, that someone would be Cousin Basil's sister, who lived with him. Being Cousin Basil's sister, she was, of course, Amelia's cousin as well. Her name was Cousin Charlotte.

It was Cousin Charlotte who now sat in the cab with Amelia on the terrible ride to the train that would take her to the ship that was to transport her across the ocean. And every beat of the horses' hooves carried her farther and farther from what she loved most—to what? Was it not likely that Cousin Basil, being brother to Cousin Charlotte, might be her very image? Amelia turned her head slightly, not wanting to stare rudely, and looked at Cousin Charlotte from the corners of her eyes. What she saw only brought back the cold knot in her stomach that she had felt when they first met. Then, instead of taking Amelia in her arms, Cousin Charlotte had held out a cold, lifeless hand that barely touched Amelia's own, so shyly, warmly, and hopefully stretched out to her.

Since Cousin Charlotte now sat staring stiffly ahead, Amelia could not see the glacial blue eyes that had looked at her with such cruel indifference. She could, however, see the rigid chin, the bloodless cheeks, the tightly pressed lips—and the grim black hat. Oh yes, she could still see that same hat with its narrow veil dangling from the brim like a black cobweb awaiting its prey. The hat somehow managed to imprison all of Cousin Charlotte's hair so that not a shred of it escaped anywhere. And Amelia had yet to see her without this dread black headpiece.

Amelia only gazed at her for one chilling moment, but she must have felt she was being spied upon, for to Amelia's dismay, she slowly turned her head. Amelia felt her face flush as she awaited a reprimand for her rudeness. Instead, after a few painful moments had passed, Cousin Charlotte abruptly turned her face away and began to speak in a flat, curiously harsh voice.

"This is as good a time as any to inform you that this journey is not one I desired to make. For this there are a number of reasons, only one of which need concern you. That one is that I do not travel well by any mode of transportation. Now I have discovered that I particularly do not travel well by ship. As I see no reason to believe that there will be any improvement on this return voyage, I may frequently wish to retire to the cabin, leaving you on your own. I have been assured by your school and by Mrs. Charlton that you are a good and obedient child. Is that so?"

"I . . . I pray so, Cousin Charlotte," Amelia replied.

"I pray so too, for your sake," said Cousin Charlotte. "In any event, whether I am present or not, I shall expect you to keep quietly to yourself at all times. Is that clear?"

"Yes, Cousin Charlotte," replied Amelia, for it was very clear indeed. She was, in plain words, always to remember that she was Cousin Charlotte's prisoner, and to behave accordingly. But Cousin Charlotte had nothing to fear. For Amelia would not for all the world have proved Aunt Felicia or Mrs. Draper false by not being the "good and obedient" child they had said she was. She fully intended to do exactly as requested by Cousin Charlotte.

In truth, however, though she felt sorry that Cousin Charlotte would find no "improvement" on this return voyage, Amelia could not feel sorry that she would not have Cousin Charlotte as her companion every waking hour. Nor did she mind that she had to keep to herself. For in her portmanteau she had put two of her favorite books, her doll Gwendolyn, and her needlework, a reticule she was embroidering for Aunt Felicia. And with whom on that ship would she have wanted to be anyway? The people she most loved in the world were left behind or gone forever.

"Have you any questions?" asked Cousin Charlotte sharply.

Questions? Oh yes, Amelia had dozens of questions. She hesitated a moment. "None, Cousin Charlotte," she replied, for was that not the answer expected of her?

"Very well then, we understand each other," said Cousin Charlotte. Then she muttered through tight lips, more to herself than to Amelia it seemed, "I have charged myself with seeing that you are delivered safely, and delivered safely you shall be." After that she lapsed again into silence, saying not one word more until they arrived at the station, where they were to embark on the train that would take them to their ship.

Delivered, Amelia thought, like a parcel—an unwanted parcel! For she was yet to be told that her presence was desired by anyone with whom she was to live. It was already becoming clear that she was no more than a burden to them. Did they think that for some reason they *must* take her in? And why did they even feel that Cousin Charlotte, who was made ill by travel, *had* to come for her? Why could Polly not have been her traveling companion, as she would have been willing to be? How could Amelia bear to live in a place where she was only being cared for as an unpleasant, unwanted duty?

Hoping Cousin Charlotte would not notice, Amelia put a hand inside her coat and closed her fingers around her gold locket, which she was wearing. How was it possible that such a person as the one sitting in the cab with her had any connection with the sweet face that was Mama's, pictured inside the locket? Was it possible that this cousin was not her cousin after all? Might not a letter come telling Amelia that some dreadful mistake had been made, and that some other person of the very same name was her true cousin? That person would surely have to be better than this one, for how was it possible that one could be worse? Amelia knew she would be praying night and day for such a letter to come. It was indeed her only hope as she sat locked in the dark cab with the stone-cold person who, until such a letter came, she would have to consider as her cousin—her Cousin Charlotte.

Chapter II

Alone

If Amelia had felt frightened at any time during the dismal cab and train ride to the dock, it was nothing to the way she felt when they finally arrived there. As Cousin Charlotte made arrangements for a porter to carry their luggage aboard the ship, Amelia stood on the dock beside her steamer trunk, her portmanteau, and Cousin Charlotte's carpetbag, looking up at the SS *Sylvania*. Surely it was a mistake that such an elegant-sounding name should have been given to the big, dark hulk looming over her. Even the lamps swinging on the decks only served to make it look more eerie and threatening. And whereas on the cab and train she could still hope that she could somehow jump off and make her way back to Aunt Felicia and Polly, there could be no such hope once she boarded the ship. They were to set sail early in the morning, and there would be miles and miles of fathoms-deep water all around them. There could be no thoughts of jumping off then!

All around them were noise and confusion. Ship's crewmen shouted to burly longshoremen as they loaded provisions onto the ship. Clusters of passengers, each one seeming to believe that his or her requirements should receive first attention, fussed and fretted over their great piles of luggage. A small child standing nearby with its parents began to wail heartrendingly from weariness and fright. It was, all told, a cheerless and foreboding scene.

But then Amelia suddenly saw something that for several minutes caused her to forget everything around her—the crewmen and dockworkers, the fretting passengers, the wailing child—everything, including the menacing presence of the dark ship itself. For her attention was now fixed on four people standing some distance beyond where she herself stood. They were too far off for Amelia to know what they might be saying to one another, but as they stood almost directly under a large hanging oil lantern, she had a clear view of all four.

One of them was in a white cap and dark suit with brass buttons, a uniform, most certainly, of the ship's captain. The remaining three people were dressed in a rather startling manner, at least compared to the other passengers. One of the three, a somewhat heavyset man of medium height, wore a top hat, striped trousers, and a swallow-tailed coat with a prodigious white blossom in the buttonhole. No other gentleman passenger wore anything that even distantly resembled this costume.

His appearance, however, paled in comparison to that of the second man. Thinner, taller, and younger looking, he was wearing a handsome military uniform with red cap, black trousers, and a white jacket topped with a dashing short red cape. The jacket and cap were decorated with an extraordinary number of rows of gold braid that picked up glints of light from the lantern overhead, as did an equally extraordinary number of rows of medals across his chest.

Still, it was the fourth member of this group that most caught Amelia's attention. She was a young girl about Amelia's own height, and perhaps even her own age. The girl wore white mittens, white high-button shoes, and a bright sapphire-blue coat, which flared out from her waist to such a degree that it seemed she must have been wearing not only a dress under it but a dozen petticoats as well. Every time she moved, her coat rippled out around her. But what was most captivating to Amelia was the young girl's hair, long golden curls that floated rather than hung over her shoulders. And atop these curls was, no, not a hat, but a tiara of twinkling diamonds. A tiara! That could mean only one thing—she was a princess!

Still, there were two things about these people that were puzzling. Should a princess not be attended by some maids-in-waiting? The only people around the captain and the royal persons were groups of pitifully shabby people clutching bundles and string-tied boxes as they made their way to a second gangplank at the rear of the ship. These were not at all like the fashionably dressed people with their piles of costly luggage nearer to Amelia. And most certainly there was not one among them who could pass for a lady-in-waiting.

Another puzzle was this: Where one would have expected the captain to be saluting and bowing to the royal persons, what actually was happening was quite the opposite. The top-hatted gentleman would make a low bow, as if the weight of the blossom in his buttonhole were pulling him down. Then the military gentleman would salute smartly. And finally, with her sapphire-blue coat and golden curls billowing out, the princess would make a curtsy. A few words would be exchanged with the captain, and then once again there would be a bow, salute, and curtsy. Bow, salute, curtsy. Bow, salute, curtsy. They bobbed up and down like mechanical windup toys, but were somehow so enchanting they made Amelia feel as if she had been carried off into a fairy-tale world.

"Amelia! What are you gawking at?"

Cousin Charlotte's sharp voice snatched her instantly back to her real world. She felt her cheeks flush, for she knew she was guilty of bad manners in staring as she had. Still, she was hardly prepared for the look on Cousin Charlotte's face, for her eyes were flaring, her nose and lips pinched with fury. One corner of her mouth twitched as if she were having difficulty containing her rage.

"I ... I ... I was looking at the young girl," Amelia stammered. And then, before she stopped to think, she burst out, "I ... I ... I do believe she is a ... a ... "

"Never mind what she is! She is no concern of yours," snapped Cousin Charlotte. "But if she should be traveling on our ship, I expect you to have nothing to do with her. Do you understand?"

Have nothing to do with a princess? What if she should smile at Amelia? Was Amelia not permitted to smile back? The order seemed to come out of pure meanness. But being "a good and obedient child," there was nothing Amelia could say, nor would she have dared. For to tell the truth, her cousin had begun to frighten her.

"Yes, Cousin Charlotte," she replied. Then, without looking back once, she followed her cousin up the gangplank into the dark, hulking ship.

Moments later they entered a room of unimaginable splendor! Who could know that this great ship, looming over the docks in such a threatening manner in the night, held such a room?

"This is the grand saloon," announced the ship's steward who was escorting them with their baggage. And grand it was indeed!

The room was bathed in the soft glow of oil lamps hanging in elegant bronze holders from walls paneled in gleaming walnut. Rich velvet chairs of deep blue and royal purple rested on thick oriental carpets. Sparkling mirrors were everywhere—on the walls, on the doors, and even on the great columns that rose to the ceiling—every one set in bronze enchantingly fashioned into shells and other fanciful shapes representing the sea. And the flickering lights of every lamp were reflected again and again in all the mirrors. It was a room fit for any princess who might be traveling on that ship!

A few passengers were seated in the grand saloon in small cozy groups. They appeared to have left behind on the dock all their cares and worries about their baggage, chatting to one another in a lively, cheerful manner as if they had found old friends aboard or were busy making new ones.

But Cousin Charlotte seemed to have no interest in the splendid room or anyone in it. She strode through the grand saloon, her black hat sitting severely on her head, her black handbag clutched tightly in her hands, her eyes deadbolted to the back of the ship's steward. If she noticed anything around her, it was impossible to tell. She seemed intent only on arriving at her cabin.

Her cabin! Was *her* cabin to be Amelia's cabin as well? As an only child, Amelia had never shared a room with anyone in her life. Was she now to share one with the last person in the world she would have chosen as a roommate—Cousin Charlotte?

Leaving the grand saloon, the dismal little parade marched resolutely down a long corridor lined with closed doors. Some bore gleaming miniature brass plates lettered with the words "toilette." Other brass plates announced that behind the door one would find a bath, to be reserved when needed, the steward informed them. Most doors, however, were simply numbered, and it was before one of these that the steward stopped and unlocked the door. The cabin they entered, with a bed built in to each of opposite walls, was clearly intended for two people. The steward set down the bags, handed Cousin Charlotte the keys to the cabin, and then turned to leave.

"I hope you and the young miss enjoy your voyage, madam," he said, smiling.

"Thank you," replied Cousin Charlotte stiffly. "But I should appreciate your taking Miss Fairwick's bag into the cabin reserved next to this one. Her room number is clearly marked on it, I believe."

So Amelia was to have her own cabin after all! Although she

was sorry for the steward's discomfiture, it was all she could do to keep from showing her relief. But with her face quite, quite expressionless, she followed Cousin Charlotte and the steward to the cabin next door. There, with a face now equally expressionless, the steward announced that breakfast would be served in the dining saloon at eight, and to ring for him if needed. Then he quickly departed.

But in the cabin he left behind, there was to be no removing of coats and hats, nor a sit-down for a cozy, comforting chat. Cousin Charlotte simply looked around the cabin, then pursed her lips. "Well, this matter being settled, I believe we should now retire. I shall expect you at my door precisely at eight, the hour at which breakfast is served. Were you provided with a pocket watch?"

"Yes," replied Amelia. "I . . . I have one in my portmanteau."

"And will there be anything else you need before then?" Cousin Charlotte asked.

"No, nothing, thank you, Cousin Charlotte," said Amelia.

"Then I will bid you good night," she replied.

A moment later, Amelia stood alone in her cabin. Alone in her cabin. Alone on the ship. To all intents and purposes, alone in the world. But she must not think about that. She must not! There was nothing to be gained by it—shedding tears over it.

But when she turned down the oil lamp, its flickering light seemed to have taken all her brave resolutions right along with it. She lay in her bed in the dark—tired, alone, and frightened. She was in a small room that looked and felt, and even smelled strange, somewhere in the middle of a ship that, for all its grandeur, was still terrifying—a ship that was carrying her away from all that she had known and loved. Curled up in a tight ball, she clasped her hands together tightly to keep from trembling, but she could not keep the scalding tears from pouring down her cheeks. At last, she turned over and threw her face into her pillow.

Faint rustling sounds had come from the cabins on either side of her, one containing strangers, the other containing a cold-blooded stranger with a name—Cousin Charlotte. But who of them knew—or even cared—that in the cabin between them a young girl lay sobbing?

Chapter III

A Real Princess

Crick, cree-ee-ee-eak. Crick, cree-ee-ee-eak.

The sounds wove their way through Amelia's dream. They seemed to come from the twisted branch of a bare tree holding a swing. Amelia was in the swing, going slowly, slowly up, and slowly back again. In front of her, in the distance, she could barely see three people, Papa, Aunt Felicia, and Polly, all smiling, with arms outstretched as if waiting for Amelia to come to them. Why, oh why, did the swing not stop so she could jump off and run to them? Who was pushing it? Turning her head, she saw a ghostly figure with arms stiffly forward, its face hidden in the shadows of a deadly black hat.

"Stop! Stop! Stop!" Amelia cried. But the figure never dropped its arms. It just stood there waiting for the swing to return to be pushed yet again. "Stop! Stop! Stop!" Amelia sobbed, and at last the sound of her voice crying woke her up.

But she almost felt as if she were still in her dream. Where was she? What was this strange little room she was in? Why had the creaking sounds not stopped with the dream? And why was the room slowly rolling back and forth, making her feel as if she were still on the swing? And then all at once she remembered. Slowly,

15

carefully, she peeled back her coverlet and crawled on her hands and knees to peer out the small round window over her bed.

What met her eyes was miles and miles of bleak grey water, stretching out in great rolling waves until it reached the sky that hung menacingly over it like a great grey bowl. It was impossible to tell where the water ended and the sky began. Close by, directly under the window, the water was rushing by, sending out streams of raging white foam. There was no sign of land anywhere. The ship had set sail early that morning as promised, and they were now far out to sea. Amelia drew her arms tightly about herself, shivering.

And just then she remembered something else. Quickly scrambling down from her bed, she unfastened her portmanteau, and drew from it her small gold pocket watch. Snapping open the lid, she saw that it was but a few minutes before eight. "Precisely at eight," she had been told, and she was not yet dressed! How was she to manage getting dressed on a floor that insisted on tilting one way and then another, with the walls all around groaning as if the cabin had every intention of breaking into splinters? But dress she must, so with shaking fingers she began to clamber into her clothes. Then, fearful that at any moment she might run into Cousin Charlotte coming from her cabin, Amelia made a hurried visit to one of the rooms with the small brass plates on the door. And, oh, how grateful she was that she could quickly return to complete getting ready at the pretty little brass basin in her own cabin. Still, another look at her pocket watch told her that she had only moments to spare when she finally slipped from her cabin. Outside Cousin Charlotte's door, she hesitated a moment to gather courage, before raising a timid hand to knock. The ship had no more than rolled from side to side twice when the door swung open. Amelia could not hold back a sharp gasp.

Cousin Charlotte's face was so drained of color it might have passed as cold white marble. And although no longer in her grim black coat, she was in a black dress equally grim, adorned only by a glaringly ugly black garnet brooch at the neck. And on her head, most curiously—most horribly—was the same familiar black hat. She might, in truth, have been the ghastly apparition that appeared in Amelia's nightmare!

"As you can no doubt see, Amelia, I am unwell," she said. "I will, therefore, not be accompanying you to the dining saloon this morning. I am certain, however, that you can find your way there. You must wait at the door, and the steward will show you to your assigned seat. There will be others at your table, so I must remind you again that you are to speak only when necessary for politeness sake, and later keep to yourself. Is that understood?"

"Yes, Cousin Charlotte," replied Amelia, finally collecting herself enough to remember her manners. "I . . . I am sorry to know that you are unwell."

"It was not unexpected," Cousin Charlotte replied in a dead voice. "I assure you, however, that I will be present at the noonday meal. I will expect you to report to my cabin at that time. Now, have you any questions?"

"N . . . none, Cousin Charlotte," said Amelia.

"Then you may go now." The door clicked shut, and Amelia found herself alone once again.

Hanging on to the brass rail to steady herself, she started off down the corridor. Much as she did not wish to be in the company of Cousin Charlotte, it was frightening to be completely on her own. When she finally arrived at the vast dining room, she felt timid and shy standing in the wide doorway. The room was filled with long tables draped in sparkling white tablecloths. Around the tables stood rows of handsome red-plush swivel chairs, their seats decorated with gleaming gold fringes that swayed with the motion of the ship. The room hummed with the voices of passengers already seated at the long tables.

Fortunately, a smiling steward soon approached her. "Name, miss?"

"A . . . A . . . Amelia Fairwick," stammered Amelia.

"This way then, miss," the steward said. "Will you be taking breakfast by yourself this morning?"

"Oh yes," replied Amelia. Then, warming to his smile, she added eagerly, "My . . . my cousin would be with me, but she is feeling unwell."

"I'm sorry to hear that, miss," said the steward. "The seas are a bit heavy this morning, but the captain does expect it to settle down a bit later today. Perhaps then it will be pleasant enough to promenade on deck."

To these remarks, Amelia only nodded, for she had suddenly remembered Cousin Charlotte's warning. Amelia was to keep to herself, and speak as little as possible to anyone. Yet here she was, the first time on her own, having far more of a conversation than she ought. She must learn to be more careful.

As it turned out, she had little cause to worry, that morning at least. Next to the seat to which she was ushered was an empty one, presumably reserved for Cousin Charlotte. As for the red-plush chair to the other side of her, it was occupied by an elderly gentleman who was far more interested in his boiled egg and toast than in talking to Amelia. Nor did there seem to be anyone else close by interested in trying to make conversation with a child, especially one who seemed unable to do more than say "yes" or "no" when asked a question.

There were no other children in the dining saloon, at least none that were more than babies. Yet what difference would it have made if there had been? Cousin Charlotte would no more have allowed Amelia to have anything to do with them than she would have the princess. The princess, of course, was not in the dining saloon either. That was disappointing but not unexpected, for would not a princess be having breakfast served to her in her royal cabin?

Amelia's own dull breakfast over, she could hardly wait to

return to her cabin and pull from her portmanteau the things that were dear and familiar to her—her doll, a favorite book, and her needlework. But no more than two hours later, Amelia began to feel that she was imprisoned in the cabin. She wondered how she could bear to be held there all those many days to be spent in crossing the ocean. Should she venture out to the grand saloon? Might she not feel just as lonely and uncomfortable there as she had in the dining saloon? And then, suddenly, she remembered what the steward had said, "Perhaps then it will be pleasant enough to promenade on deck." Well, pleasant or not, it could not be so bad that she should not at least attempt it. And she did not, after all, have to knock on Cousin Charlotte's door until noon. Moments later, Amelia had on her grey woolen coat, and had her matching grey bonnet tied firmly under her chin. Then, following the signs, she made her way down the swaying corridor to the door that led to the deck.

As soon as she opened the door, she was met by a brisk, fresh wind in her face, the tangy smell of salt air, and the sound of the waves rushing past the ship. It was so startling that her first thought was to scurry back into the safety of the corridor. But, after hesitating a moment, she ran across the deck instead. Then, holding her breath, she stood on tiptoes and peered over the iron rail to have a better look at the water racing by far beneath her.

"It is quite exciting, is it not?"

Amelia started, turning quickly to see a tall, thin man, his face sallow and heavily bearded, standing behind her. He had approached so silently, she had not heard any footsteps.

"I beg your pardon if I startled you," the man said. "My name is Mr. Pymm. And yours is . . . ?"

"A . . . A . . . Amelia Fairwick," stammered Amelia, who though warned to keep to herself, also knew she must be polite and reply.

"Ah yes, Miss Fairwick," Mr. Pymm repeated softly. "The water is beautiful, don't you agree?"

As Amelia nodded hesitantly, Mr. Pymm came closer and leaned on the railing beside her. "Bubbles swirling by like little water fairies. Spray dancing to the music of the sea. What a pity it is that we must be so far above it." Mr. Pymm's gentle, dreamy voice seemed to blend in with the sound of the water rushing by down below them.

Bubbles like water fairies! Dancing spray! How lovely it sounded. Mr. Pymm was right; it was a pity to be so far above it. Suddenly, Amelia felt she must be closer. She swiftly stepped onto a ledge halfway up the railing and leaned way over.

"What do you think you're doing? Sir, can't you see that girl is about to topple into the sea?" a voice cried out.

Amelia very nearly did topple, but only onto the deck as she dropped off the ledge and whirled around. "Oh! Oh!" she gasped.

She barely heard Mr. Pymm's voice as he said, "My apologies indeed, but the young lady was perfectly safe . . . perfectly safe, quite surely. And now I bid you good morning!" His footsteps tapped softly away down the deck and, mingling with the sound of the rushing water, soon vanished.

With a wildly thumping heart, Amelia dropped a deep curtsy. "Your . . . your royal highness!" she breathed. For standing before her was the princess!

She was not wearing her tiara, but she was dressed in the same sapphire-blue coat. Her golden hair now billowed out from under a blue bonnet decorated with an enormous pink ostrich feather that curled over the crown. A wide pink satin ribbon tied under her chin kept this grand affair from flying off in the wind.

Her royal highness stood for a moment studying Amelia with a curious look that rapidly moved from surprise to suspicion, and finally to amusement. At last, she honored Amelia with a wide grin. "That was nice," she said, and waved a royal arm imperiously. "You may do it again."

Hardly believing that anything so thrilling could be happening to her, the delighted Amelia dropped an even deeper curtsy.

To this, the princess tilted her head and studied Amelia with halfway narrowed eyes. "How did you know I was a . . . a royal highness?"

"I saw you last night, and you had on a tiara, or perhaps it was a crown. I guessed right away you were a princess," Amelia said proudly. Then, anxious to further display her great cleverness, she rushed on excitedly. "Then I guessed that the military gentleman must be your royal guard. And the other gentleman, the one in the top hat, must be your prime minister."

"Oh, aren't you a clever girl!" said the princess. "What's your name?"

"Amelia Fairwick," replied Amelia.

"Well," said the princess, "I am . . . I am Princess Primrose Lagoon."

"Should I call you Princess Lagoon or Princess Primrose?" asked Amelia shyly.

"Oh, you can just call me Princess," her royal highness replied with an airy wave of her hand.

"Thank you, P . . . Princess," said Amelia, her cheeks grown warm with pleasure. "You know, even though I saw you last night, I didn't think you were on the ship, because you weren't in the dining saloon at breakfast. But then, I . . . I expect you were having it in your royal stateroom."

"Yes, I expect I was," replied the princess. Then, after barely a moment's pause, she asked abruptly, "What did they give you to eat?"

This seemed like a very curious thing for the princess to ask, but Amelia was far too polite to mention it. "Oh, we had lots of things to choose from," she replied.

"Like what?" asked the princess.

"Well," said Amelia, having to think about it a moment, "The gentleman next to me had an egg and toast. I had a hot muffin with butter and honey, a cup of milk, and an apple."

"Creepers!" said the princess.

And small wonder, for she must have thought this the most ordinary fare. "What . . . what did you have?" asked Amelia.

"Oh, all sorts of things," replied the princess with an imperious toss of her beribboned chin. Then all at once, with no warning, she announced, "I have to go now. I wouldn't want them to find me out. I'm not supposed to be here, you understand."

Amelia nodded eagerly. This was all very exciting, being part of the princess's escape from the watchful eyes of her royal guardians. "But . . ." Amelia hesitated, wondering if it was proper for her to ask. "But will I see you again, your royal highness?"

"I expect you will," replied her royal highness. "You'll likely see me tonight, though not to talk to. But if I can manage it, we can meet here tomorrow at the same time. Anyway, I'm off for now."

With a breezy little wave of her hand, she started down the deck. But she did not get far before she stopped suddenly, wheeled around, and looked back at Amelia. "Could you bring me an apple tomorrow?" This sounded less like a polite request than it did a royal command.

"Oh yes!" breathed Amelia. It did not seem at all remarkable to her that a princess, who might ordinarily breakfast on something like out-of-season strawberries under golden glass, might want a common apple. For was this not simply a royal whim? Better yet, was not the princess having to come to collect her apple a promise that she would be back to meet with Amelia the next day?

Now, in the matter of only a few minutes, this journey across the ocean did not seem so terrible. What was to come at the end of it, Amelia would try not to think about. For now, she could look forward not only to the meeting the next day, but the mysterious appearance of the princess that very night. Could it be that she might actually be going to have her evening meal in the dining saloon with her royal attendants?

Amelia was so excited over the recent turn of events that it was not until she had left the deck and was returning to her cabin that she remembered the warning given her only the night before. How, oh how, could she have forgotten it? This was not a general warning to keep to herself and speak only when necessary. No, this was a very special warning, directed at one special person—the princess. "If she should be traveling on our ship, I expect you to have nothing to do with her." Oh yes, these were the exact cold, deadly words of Cousin Charlotte!

Chapter IV

A Surprise Performance

Her face as deathly pale and sickly as it had been that morning, Cousin Charlotte marched grimly with Amelia to their noonday meal in the dining saloon. She wore not only the same stark black dress with the ugly garnet brooch, but curiously, the same black hat, complete with narrow black cobweb veil. Was she never to appear without that forbidding headpiece?

As for the meal itself, other than having Cousin Charlotte's dark presence beside her, it turned out to be no different for Amelia than the one she had had by herself. Cousin Charlotte, while doing no more than tasting a crust of bread and sipping a cup of tea, made no attempt to have a conversation with anyone, and rebuffed every attempt at conversation with her. It must have been clear to all that she wished to be left alone, and so she was. Everyone had, of course, given up attempts at conversation with Amelia. So the two sat there together in the dining saloon in deadly silence.

The evening meal was no better, the only difference being that Amelia's heart was beating faster, for had Princess Primrose Lagoon not said that Amelia would likely see her that very night? Where else could that be but in the dining saloon? Yet despite

Amelia's many secret glances around the room, there was no princess anywhere to be seen. As the meal wore on, it became clearer and clearer that she was not to put in an appearance. Amelia's spirits sank lower and lower as she sat nibbling her bread pudding at the end of the meal.

Then all at once a flurry of activity took place at the wide doorway into the dining saloon. The captain quickly sprang to his feet and began tapping his tea cup with a spoon.

"May I have your attention, please! I am happy to announce that we have with us members of the London stage, who have kindly agreed to honor us with a program of recitation and song. Allow me to present to you first, Mr. Thessalonius Smeech!"

Heads turned, chairs swiveled, and the dining saloon rang with applause as in through the doorway appeared a heavyset man in top hat and swallow-tailed coat, with a great white blossom in the buttonhole. Beaming, he took off his hat with a great flourish and bowed to all the passengers. He was, of course, one of the very same three people Amelia had seen on the dock the night before!

"Next, we have Mr. Alphonso Turk!" announced the captain, as the younger man in the splendid military uniform marched smartly through the doorway, saluted, and bowed.

"Finally," said the captain, "we have the little London canary and actress—Miss Primrose Lagoon!"

And through the doorway tripped Amelia's princess! As she curtsied to the right and to the left, the half dozen petticoats under the skirt of her pink velveteen dress flew up most deliciously around her, clearly delighting the audience.

Upon seeing her, Amelia's feelings turned from shock to terrible disappointment to burning indignation. Princess, indeed! How dared this girl, this—this Primrose person, pretend to be a princess! But as the three "members of the London stage" threaded their way around the tables in a small parade to the back of the dining saloon, it took but a few more moments for Amelia to remember that it was she herself who had dropped a deep curtsy and addressed this "little London canary" as "your royal highness." Then, terribly pleased with herself, she had rushed on to say, "I guessed right away you were a princess."

Now, what would a clever young actress do when presented with this golden opportunity? Might she not just decide to play the part of the princess for the simpleton who had given her the idea? Amelia had no one to blame but herself. Tomorrow, when they met, there would be nothing to do but laugh about it.

When they met! Yet how could they meet when Amelia had now remembered Cousin Charlotte's warning? How "good and obedient" would she be if she were to disobey Cousin Charlotte? Amelia gave her a swift, sidelong glance, but saw no expression on her face whatsoever. And so she sat, rigid and motionless, through-out the entire performance. This turned out to be so thrilling for Amelia, she soon was able to forget the grim presence beside her.

Mr. Thessalonius Smeech was the first to entertain the assem-bled passengers, starting off with what Amelia thought were the funniest jokes she had ever heard.

"The other day," said Mr. Smeech, leaning over to draw a deep breath from what was clearly only a paper flower in his buttonhole, "I asked Mrs. Squiggs how her husband was, and this is what she replied, 'Why, the doctor said that if he lives until morning, we shall have some hopes of him, but if he doesn't, we must give him up!'"

Before the laughter had quite died down, Mr. Smeech went on, "I said to my friend the other day that London was certainly the foggiest place in the world. 'Oh no,' said he, 'it's not. I've been in a place much foggier than London.' 'Where was that?' I asked. 'I don't know where it was,' replied my friend, 'it was so foggy!'

"And you know," continued Mr. Smeech, "the wife of that same friend, going out for the day, left a card on the back door for the grocer's benefit. 'All out,' it read. 'Don't leave anything.' On her return, she found her house ransacked and all her choicest possessions gone. To the card on the door was added, 'Thanks. We haven't left much.'

"But I have to tell you," said Mr. Smeech, drolly shaking his head, "that this morning one of the passengers on this ship said to me, 'So you are an actor. Well, I am a banker, and I think it must be at least fifteen years since I was at a theatre.' 'Oh, that's all right,' I replied, 'I'm quite certain it's at least fifteen years since I was at a bank!'"

Oh, how Amelia laughed at these stories, and again when Mr. Smeech recited "Father William" from one of her very favorite books, a copy of which was in her cabin at that very moment. The recitation had no sooner ended when Mr. Smeech bowed and sat down, to be replaced by Mr. Alphonso Turk, who came bounding out from a corner where he had been waiting.

Then the laughter soon turned to a deep silence filled with suspense and dread as Mr. Turk recited the solemn words of "Casabianca." His arms raised, then dropped to his sides with fists clenched. His head raised, eyes rolled heavenward, and then suddenly drooped on his chest.

> "The boy stood on the burning deck,
>   Whence all but he had fled;
>   The flame that lit the battle's wreck
>   Shone round him o'er the dead."

This was both thrilling and horrifying at the same time. Amelia felt goose bumps rising on her neck. Then, only moments later, "Casabianca" ended, and tears rolled down her cheeks as Mr. Turk delivered the words of "The Little Orphans."

> " 'Let us go, my little brother,'
>   Said a voice so low and sweet
>   That I held my breath to listen

Till I heard my heart string beat.
'Let us go, my little brother,
To the churchyard, you and I.
Thinking all the time of mother,
Let us on the daisies lie.' "

A hush fell over the assembled passengers when the sad words of the poem ended. Then the dining saloon rang with their applause. There was even more applause as the little London canary, Primrose Lagoon, skipped lightly out, curtsying to the audience as Mr. Turk bowed himself off to one side, and Mr. Smeech sat himself down at a piano safely bolted to the back wall of the dining saloon. He struck a few crashing chords while Primrose Lagoon established a soulful look on her face and stretched her arms out to the audience.

"Believe me if all those endearing young charms
Which I gaze on so fondly today,
Were to change by tomorrow and fleet in my arms
Like the fairy gifts fading away."

Primrose trilled.

When she finished the song, the applause was thunderous, for the London canary was clearly the most popular of the performers that evening. She then fluted "The Last Rose of Summer" and sweetly warbled the words of "Drink To Me Only With Thine Eyes."

This last, to Amelia's immense disappointment, signaled the end of the performance. After the captain thanked them wholeheartedly and promised the audience that there would be at least one more performance before the end of the voyage, the members of the London stage trooped out of the dining saloon.

The passengers then all rose to leave as well, among them

Amelia and Cousin Charlotte, who had sat through the whole performance as if carved in stone. She had neither smiled nor shed a tear, nor even applauded faintly. Perhaps she would say nothing about it, and nothing further about Primrose.

But as they marched to their cabins in deadly silence, Cousin Charlotte suddenly began to speak. "I shall advise the steward to inform me in advance if there is to be further entertainment of that sort planned for the passengers. We will then dine early and leave before it begins. But we will *not* be subject to such a thing again. Furthermore, Amelia, you *do* recollect my warning to you regarding that girl, do you not?"

"Y . . . y . . . yes, Cousin Charlotte," said Amelia, her voice trembling.

"Well, see that you do," said Cousin Charlotte, and swept into her cabin, shutting the door with a sharp click of the lock.

The sound of it seemed to linger in the air, a reminder to Amelia that locked away in that cabin was any hope of a meeting with Primrose Lagoon, laughing together over Amelia's grand thoughts of royalty and princesses, and most certainly locked away were any thoughts of presenting that precious apple!

Chapter V

Explanations

Slowly, carefully, barely breathing, Amelia let herself out of her cabin and tiptoed down the corridor. Buried deep in the pocket of her coat was a beautiful, perfectly round red apple, polished by a bit of petticoat until it gleamed.

Amelia was definitely not going to give this apple to anyone. Nor was she going out on the deck to meet with someone. Oh no, not at all! She was simply going out on deck for some fresh air and to look over the railing. Most carefully, of course! But if someone should happen to come along, Amelia could hardly be so rude as not to speak when spoken to, now could she?

As for the apple, why she would just lay that down on the deck, or perch it on the railing for some hungry seagull to find. The fact that she had had to slip the apple *secretly* from the fruit bowl in the dining saloon and then into her dress pocket, she would not think about. After all, if Cousin Charlotte, sitting beside her, had caught her at it, she would have been quite honest about what she intended to do with the apple, even though she feared there was not much likelihood Cousin Charlotte would believe the story about the seagull.

The apple was still in her pocket as she stood at the railing trying to give all her attention to the bubbles and spray below her, and particularly trying not to look over her shoulder to see who might be coming down the deck toward her. After all, she was not waiting for anyone. No, not at all! And then at last she heard the voice she absolutely did *not* expect to hear.

"I thought you might of decided not to come," it said.

Amelia instantly spun around, pretending to herself to be surprised at seeing Primrose standing there, complete with sapphire-blue coat and feathered hat. But there *was* one surprise that took no pretending at all, for suddenly Amelia saw how worn the sapphire-blue coat really was, and how short were the sleeves that displayed far too much of a pair of pale thin wrists. It was painfully clear that the owner of the coat had long since outgrown it. As for the grand hat, how skinny and sparse the ostrich feather now appeared, how spotted the pink ribbon, and how frayed it was where it had been tied too many times under the chin. How, Amelia wondered, could she have ever believed that a princess wore this shabby costume—costume, in truth, being what it could rightly be called?

"Why ever wouldn't I come?" Amelia said, rather defiantly.

"Because I'm no creeping princess like you thought," replied Primrose. Then she added, equally defiantly, "Course it's not my fault you thought that."

"No one ever said it was. *I* was the one that was a simpleton to think so," said Amelia.

Primrose's bright blue eyes, already of large proportions, grew even larger at this. She was astonished, it seemed, that there was to be no argument about the matter. "Well, all right then. But . . . but did you bring me my apple?"

Amelia hesitated. She had begun to think that she should have laid the apple down someplace for "the seagull" as she had planned to do. For how could she explain a silly story like *that* to Primrose if she were to do it now? Still, she reasoned quickly, Primrose *was* a bird of sorts, a canary to be sure and not a seagull, but a bird nonetheless. So perhaps that made it all right after all.

"Forgot it, didn't you? Figured you would," said Primrose with a toss of her outrageous bonnet.

"No, I did not!" said Amelia indignantly. She pulled the apple from her pocket. "Here it is!"

Primrose took the apple from Amelia's hand and instantly thrust it into her pocket. But after thinking this over a moment, she pulled it back out. "Might as well eat it now," she muttered. "If Smeech or Turk or anyone else down there finds it, I'll never get so much as the seeds." With that, she took a huge, unladylike bite of the apple.

"Can't . . . can't you get an apple anytime you like?" asked Amelia.

"In the creeping steerage?" Primrose nearly exploded. "Not likely! Why ever did you think I asked for one?"

Amelia did not think her reasons for thinking that were worthy of explanation, so she simply shook her head. "But . . . but what's steerage?" she asked.

"Might of guessed you wouldn't know," retorted Primrose. "Anyhow, there's no creeping royal staterooms there, for starters. It's the place somewhere back of the ship where they put all the people who haven't got three pence to scrape together, poor actors being among the chosen. Everyone gets crammed into one room, best described as being dark, noisy, but mostly smelly, what with half of them getting sick in all directions."

Amelia then remembered all the shabby people she had seen on the dock. Now she knew where they had been going—to the steerage. "Is that where you stay?" she asked, horrified.

"Yes and no," replied Primrose. "If you saw us on the dock, you must of seen all the whoop-de-do, me curtsying my head off, and Smeech and Turk bowing and scraping."

Amelia nodded.

"Well," said Primrose, "it was to try to get the captain to give us a first-class cabin in return for us performing. 'No cabins available,' said he, which I suspect was a creeping lie. Anyway, he said he could move us up to second cabin, which is not steerage, but close to it as a rat's tail, 'cause even though there's only eight of us in a room, we eat with the steerage. For breakfast yesterday we had bread and grease with porridge. Today we had porridge with bread and grease. We also get coffee and tea, but hard to tell which from which. Other meals not much better."

"I . . . I'm sorry," said Amelia.

"Not your fault," Primrose said. "Anyway, I'm grateful for the apple."

"Now I know why you wanted one," Amelia said. "I couldn't understand why a princess would want a plain old apple. Why did you let me go on thinking you *were* a princess?"

Primrose shrugged. "Don't know. Just thought it was fun, I suppose. Any rate, got you to bring me an apple, didn't I?"

"I would have anyway," said Amelia at once.

Primrose's startling blue eyes widened again. "You *would*?"

"Of course," replied Amelia matter-of-factly. "And . . . and I'll bring you one every day, if you like."

"Well . . . well," Primrose mumbled, clearly at a loss for words. "Well then, I'll be here. I mean, if I don't get found out."

"Doesn't your . . . your *papa* wish you to come?" asked Amelia, guessing.

"I don't have any pa, or ma either," said Primrose. "Oh, you mean Smeech or Turk, I suspect. Neither of them's my pa, or anything else. And not creeping likely they care what I do. They wouldn't care if I got fed to the creeping sharks. Well, maybe they would *now*, long as I can stay their little canary." Primrose paused a moment, a curious look clouding her face. Then she took a deep breath and went on. "It's that the ship doesn't want steerage coming up here. If they catch me, they'll likely find that someone never properly locks the iron gate between us, and I'll never get back then. Creepers! Is that a steward coming? I'd better get scarce. See you tomorrow!"

But Primrose had no more than taken two steps when she stopped and turned back. "In case you have a question in your mind about it, it's not just the apple I'm coming back for." Then she ran off down the deck, coat bouncing and pink ribbons flying in the wind. As she reached the end of the deck, the ship made an especially deep roll, and she went dancing over to one side. Then, after giving Amelia a mischievous grin over her shoulder, she rounded the bend and disappeared.

Amelia hurried back to her cabin, thoughts of all that had just happened spinning in her head. Primrose was an orphan just as she was. And she was traveling with people who would not have minded seeing her "fed to the sharks." Was that not a perfect way to describe the way Cousin Charlotte felt about Amelia? But what did Primrose mean about Mr. Smeech and Mr. Turk caring about her only as long as she stayed their little canary? Was that to be only until the end of the voyage, at which time she really would be "fed to the sharks"? This was puzzling, and frightening, too. Might Cousin Charlotte be having the same thing in mind for Amelia?

But of one thing Amelia was certain, and that was that she liked Primrose. Primrose was, in truth, a curious girl, pitiful too, in her worn outlandish costume. She was unlike anyone Amelia had known—ever. Yet, Primrose had such a jaunty, lively air about her and looked at one with such honest, forthright eyes.

Amelia determined that she was definitely going to meet with Primrose as often as she cared to, and would not even make up tales to make herself feel less wicked about doing it. Anyway, Cousin Charlotte only barely managed to appear dutifully at mealtimes to escort Amelia to the dining saloon, and never asked questions about what she did with the rest of her time. So there seemed little chance of being found out. Why bother with making up tales!

Chapter VI

A Dastardly Deed

"A boy stood on the burning deck,
   Eating apples by the peck.
His father called, he would not go,
Because he loved his apples so!"

Primrose concluded this recitation by giving Amelia a wicked grin, and then taking a great crunching, juicy bite of her apple.

Remembering how she had shed tears over Mr. Turk's moving rendition of the poem "Casabianca," Amelia did not know what to make of Primrose's version of the same poem. Somehow she felt it would be improper to smile. But Primrose looked so droll, how was it possible not to smile? "Primrose, you shouldn't do that," Amelia said, trying to keep a stern face but not at all succeeding. "What if Mr. Turk heard you?"

"Hmmmph," sniffed Primrose. "Do him good. He's so stuck on his creeping self, his nose gets bent in two when somebody doesn't note his great talents, like most of London. He didn't like it by half when Tooter said he and Smeech could have a try in America, but only if they brought the little canary along."

"Who is Tooter?" asked Amelia.

"Oh, that's Alberforce Q. Tooter, relation of some kind or other to Turk and Smeech, Turk and Smeech being likewise relations to each other. Tooter's manager of the Castle, which is a theatre no doubt one hundred times punier than it sounds. Anyway, that's where we're heading. And if you want to know . . . " Primrose stopped suddenly and peered down the deck. "Creepers! I thought someone was coming. I wish we didn't have to stand around out here on the deck in front of King Neptune and everybody."

Amelia wished that, too. Today was the fourth time they had met after that very first meeting, but the last two times Primrose had no sooner bit into her apple than a steward appeared coming down the deck, and she had flown off.

"I have some jacks and a pack of cards in my pocket, which I'm tired of playing with by myself," said Primrose. "If we had a proper place to go, we could play a game."

Amelia had never heard of jacks, nor had she ever played any card games, but she would love to show Primrose her doll Gwendolyn, and perhaps the needlework she was doing for Aunt Felicia. And both were at that very moment safely in a place that was *not* in front of King Neptune and everybody. What could be wrong with taking Primrose there?

Well, a great deal was wrong with it, and in truth Amelia knew it. But how was Cousin Charlotte to find out? After all, she never left her cabin except to visit the toilette or bath, or to escort Amelia to the dining saloon. And Amelia's meetings with Primrose had not yet been found out, had they?

"Perhaps we could go to my cabin," Amelia blurted. "You wouldn't be seen there."

"Wouldn't your ma mind?" Primrose asked.

"I don't have a mama or a papa either," said Amelia. "I . . . I'm like you. I'm an orphan."

Instead of looking sympathetic on hearing this piece of information, however, Primrose whistled and rolled her eyes. "Wheeoo!

I thought that lady with the big black hat sitting next to you in the dining saloon was your ma. Lucky for you she's not. She looked creeping scary."

"Well," said Amelia, "she . . . she's my cousin."

"Whoops!" said Primrose. "Sorry I said that then."

"It's all right," Amelia returned quickly. "She *is* scary. She's the one taking me to New York where I'm to live with my Cousin Basil. He's her brother."

"Pity for you if he's any bit like her. But I wouldn't desire to bump into her in your cabin. Brrrr!" Primrose shuddered.

"You won't," said Amelia. "We don't share a cabin. She has her own. She never comes into mine, and she doesn't need to know about it if . . . if I . . . I have a . . . a guest. She doesn't need to know about . . . anything!"

"Creepers!" breathed Primrose as they slipped stealthily into Amelia's cabin. Her eyes, widened into enormous blue O's, darted around the room, assessing everything in it. Then she quickly untied her hat, peeled off her coat, and tossed both on Amelia's bed along with her partly eaten apple. "You mean to tell me you have this cabin all to yourself?" she asked.

As she removed her own hat and coat and hung them carefully on a wall hook, Amelia nodded.

Primrose shook her head in disbelief. "Two whole beds, and one of them just going to waste. Creepers!" Then her eyes fell on something hanging on the wall close to Amelia's coat. "Whatever's *that*?"

"It's a wash basin," replied Amelia.

"A gold wash basin, and all to yourself right in your cabin!" said the astonished Primrose. "And it looks like it's even got spouts for running water!"

"It's . . . it's *not* gold," said Amelia, suddenly feeling she needed to apologize for this. "It's . . . it's only brass."

"Oh!" said Primrose, and grinned.

Amelia was beginning to feel uncomfortable. Perhaps inviting Primrose to the cabin had not been such a good idea after all. She had not considered how all this might appear to someone who had to dine in steerage on porridge and bread with grease, and was crammed into a cabin with seven other people. What would Primrose think if she were to see the elegant toilette and rose-marble bath down the corridor?

But then Primrose suddenly shrugged. "Look, it's all right. You don't have to be excusing anything. Not your fault you're rich."

"But I'm not . . . " Amelia began, and then stopped. She had never really thought about it before. She had never had to. But how was it possible to think that she was *not* rich? Look at how she was traveling, and then look at how Primrose must travel.

"Rich? Course you're rich," said Primrose matter-of-factly. She flounced out her skirt and plopped down on Amelia's bed. "Or maybe it's your cousin that's rich, and you get to enjoy the benefits." She picked up her apple and took a delicate nibble from it. "Maybe you're both rich," she went on, waving the apple around airily. "But then again, maybe it's just you that's rich, always was, and now you're an heiress. In which case, lucky cousin getting charge of you."

Amelia was not enjoying this purely one-sided conversation. She was getting sorely muddled by Primrose's ideas about who was rich and who was not, and in truth was finding the whole subject unpleasant. And after all, her situation was bad enough without adding all these complicated twists and turns. Then, to Amelia's great relief, Primrose found something else to interest her.

"Is that a locket around your neck?" she asked, pointing.

"Oh yes!" replied Amelia eagerly. She loved the locket, and was always pleased when anyone noticed it.

"Well, don't go telling me *that's* brass," said Primrose.

"N . . . n . . . no," stammered Amelia. "I . . . I expect it's gold."

"Expect nothing," said Primrose. "Course it's gold. I ought to know." She hesitated a moment. "Would you like to know how?"

Although the answer to this question was not of the greatest interest to Amelia, she nodded anyway, hoping it would not lead to another speech about how rich she was.

"If I tell you, promise you won't tell anyone?" said Primrose.

"I promise," said Amelia easily, for what person did she have to tell anything to—Cousin Charlotte? If the thought was not so frightening, Amelia might even have laughed about it.

Primrose looked nervously toward the door as if someone might be coming in. "The thing is," she said in a near whisper, "I have one as well. Course, I can't wear it like you can."

"Whyever not?" asked Amelia.

"'Cause Smeech or Turk would steal it from me," said Primrose. "They did once when I was little."

Amelia's eyes widened. "How did you ever get it back again?" she asked.

"Stole it back," replied Primrose, without so much as a flutter of her long eyelashes. "Would you like to see it?"

"Where is it now?" asked Amelia. "In your cabin?"

"Not creeping likely," replied Primrose. "I hide it on my person. You turn your back to me and close your eyes. I'll get it out."

Amelia dutifully turned around and squeezed her eyes tightly shut. Behind her she heard the soft rustling sounds of what might have been Primrose's many petticoats being lifted.

"All right to look now," Primrose said.

Amelia turned to see in Primrose's outstretched hand what was most definitely a locket of pure gold. And while oval in shape rather than round like her own, it was inscribed like hers with lacy scrollwork.

"Oh!" she breathed. "It's such a pretty locket, Primrose. Do . . . do you have a photograph in it of your mama as I do?"

Primrose nodded. "Would you like to see it as well?"

"Oh, yes!" cried Amelia softly. "And you must see mine." She quickly reached back and unfastened the chain that held her locket. Then both girls unsnapped their lockets and held them out to each other.

"Your mama was beautiful!" said Amelia. "Just like the locket."

"So was yours," said Primrose.

"Did . . . did your mama just die?" Amelia asked hesitantly.

"Oh no!" replied Primrose. "She died when I was a tiny baby."

"Mine as well," said Amelia.

For a few moments, the only sounds in the cabin came from the creaking of the ship rolling slowly back and forth, as the two girls gazed sadly at the tiny dim photographs of mothers snatched so cruelly from them when they were but infants.

At last, Primrose sighed. "I suppose I had best put my locket back where it came from. Would you turn around again, please, and close your eyes?"

Once more, Amelia did as she was instructed, and soon one locket was safely hidden on Primrose's "person" and the other safe on its chain around Amelia's neck.

"Wish I had a photo of my pa," Primrose said. "He died not long after my ma from fever. I'd of been tossed into a orphanage, then likely into the workhouse, if Mary . . . she's the costume lady . . . didn't take me on. Pa was an actor too, but he was a gentleman, not like Smeech and Turk. Mary told me so. Wish I could of stayed with her. Wish I'd never opened my creeping mouth and turned into Smeech and Turk's canary. Lucky me!" Primrose grimaced.

"My papa only just died," Amelia said. "He went away on a business journey, and he . . . he never came back. He was in a hotel fire. Lots of people were lost, and he was one of them. Now I have to go live in New York with my Cousin Basil, who is to be my guardian. Cousin Charlotte lives with him."

"In which case, looks as if you're about as lucky as me. Is she your pa's cousin?" Primrose asked.

"No, Mama's cousin," replied Amelia. "But only a very distant one."

"Miles and miles distant, if you ask me," said Primrose. "Doesn't look one bit like your ma's photo. What if she's not really your cousin? There was a play I knew once where somebody killed somebody else off, then pretended to be them. Did you ever think about something like that?"

Think about something like that? Well, had Amelia not wondered herself how someone like Cousin Charlotte could be related to her sweet mama? And had she not been praying for a letter telling her that there had been a dreadful mistake made, and that Cousin Charlotte was not her cousin after all? But *murder*? No! No! No! This was all stories and make-believe and too hideous even to think of.

"Oh no!" she cried softly, and did not want to talk about it anymore. "Would you like to play with my doll Gwendolyn?" she blurted, that being the first other subject she could think of.

Primrose wrinkled her nose. "I thought we were going to play jacks."

"I don't know how," Amelia said, "but I *would* like to learn."

Digging out the metal jacks and two small balls from her coat pocket, Primrose was down on her knees in an instant, showing Amelia how to bounce a ball and scoop up as many jacks as she could with one hand before the ball came down again. The game, it must be said, was greatly complicated by the rolling of the ship, which caused the balls to scoot all around the cabin floor in the most hilarious manner. As the girls crawled around trying to catch the balls, it seemed impossible to suppress giggles or bursts of laughter.

Amelia could not believe what a grand time she was having. Swept aside were the horrors of being in the keep of Cousin Charlotte. And swept aside, for a few moments at least, were all feelings of loneliness and unhappiness.

And then suddenly with no warning, silently and stealthily, the cabin door opened. Too late now to jump up from hands and knees. Too late now to hide bouncing balls. And oh, how especially too late to hide a half-eaten apple now prominently displayed in Primrose's hand! Once again, there was no sound in the cabin but the creaking of the ship, now become ominous sound effects for the scene being enacted.

"Creepers!" said Primrose.

For before them stood—Cousin Charlotte!

Cousin Charlotte—listening like a fox to the careless giggling and laughter of her prey on the other side of the wall.

Cousin Charlotte—stealthily observing from under her murderous black hat Amelia hiding in her pocket the apples from the breakfast table, apples now positively known to be used for a shocking, odious, despicable, dastardly, wicked, *wicked* purpose.

Cousin Charlotte—now standing in the doorway, rigid, cold, and unforgiving as a gravestone.

"How dare you, Amelia! HOW DARE YOU!"

Chapter VII

A Poor, Dear Child

A chilling fog shrouded the harbor as the big ship sliced silently through its dark, wintry water. Ooooo aaaaw! Ooooo aaaaw! How lonely and forlorn the foghorns sounded to Amelia as they sent out their warning to any ship brave enough, or perhaps foolish enough, to enter the harbor. Beware! Beware! they moaned. Beware! Beware! Standing at the railing of the ship, Amelia began to shiver. Did the foghorns have a special warning for her as well?

Oh, if only Primrose with her jaunty, cheerful air was standing there beside her. But she had not seen Primrose again since they had been found out by Cousin Charlotte. Amelia, who must only have been "masquerading" as "a good and obedient child"—Cousin Charlotte's very words—was now no longer to be trusted. So she had then, to all intents and purposes, been made a prisoner in her cabin, allowed out only for meals or to sit, wretched and miserable, in the grand saloon with Cousin Charlotte, the dreary, dismal couple neither speaking nor being spoken to.

How shameful to Amelia was the memory of poor, pitiful Primrose in her shabby coat and feathered bonnet, stuffing the balls and jacks and precious half-eaten apple into her pocket as she

43

scurried from the cabin under the cruel, forbidding eyes of Cousin Charlotte. As she left the ship by Cousin Charlotte's side, Amelia hoped desperately that she might have one last glimpse of Primrose. But she was not to be seen anywhere, and Amelia's sinking heart told her that she would never see Primrose again.

"Madam! Madam!" Amelia was startled when Mr. Pymm came hurrying up to where she and Cousin Charlotte stood awaiting the arrival of Cousin Basil, who was to come for them in a carriage. Amelia had not seen Mr. Pymm again, except from a distance, after that first time he had talked with her on the deck.

"Yes, what is it?" said Cousin Charlotte.

"I am an assistant purser from the *Sylvania*," said Mr. Pymm. "A slight problem has arisen, madam. Would you be kind enough to come a few steps this way?"

"What has it to do with?" Cousin Charlotte asked coldly.

"The young lady's steamer trunk, madam," Mr. Pymm replied. "It will take but a minute or two."

"Well, then," said Cousin Charlotte. "Please wait right here, Amelia. Do not move a step. I shall return immediately." She hesitated a moment, then picked up her carpetbag. It was as if Amelia could not be trusted to guard it for her even for a few minutes! Then she walked off, stopping on her way to give Amelia a warning look over her shoulder before following Mr. Pymm through a cluster of passengers standing nearby.

Amelia stood with hands folded, looking all around but not straying so much as an inch away. And then she saw something that caused her heart to leap. Strolling past, not twenty-five feet from where she stood, were Mr. Smeech, complete with tails, top hat, and blossom in his buttonhole, Mr. Turk in his smart military uniform, and in her outgrown sapphire-blue coat, pert bonnet with the worn pink ribbons and ratty ostrich feather, no other than—Primrose!

With Cousin Charlotte due to arrive back at any moment, and perhaps on her way now, Amelia did not dare to leave the spot where she was so firmly rooted. But she was certain Primrose had seen her. Would she run over to where Amelia stood?

Then a curious thing happened. Mr. Smeech and Mr. Turk nudged Primrose and gave her a push in Amelia's direction. But Primrose only shook her head. Amelia thought she knew why. What if Cousin Charlotte were near at hand, which in truth she was? Yet why did Mr. Smeech and Mr. Turk nudge Primrose? As far as Amelia knew, they could have no idea who she was.

At that moment, however, what meant the most to Amelia was the shy grin Primrose was giving her. Then, with hands down by her side, Primrose wiggled her fingers by way of a wave. Amelia smiled and wiggled her fingers back. So now, even though Primrose did not run over, Amelia knew that somewhere in the big, strange city she had a friend, even though petticoats bouncing up under a scruffy coat and a bedraggled pink ostrich feather drooping over her bonnet as she scrambled into a cab with the other "members of the London stage" might be the last ever seen of her.

Once again, Amelia was alone and waiting for Cousin Charlotte. Near where Amelia stood, a glaring gas lamp lit up a large clock, its sharp hands pointing like arrows at great black numbers circling its staring white face. She had not paid much attention to it, for she had had no need to do so. But now she had the uncomfortable feeling that somehow, from the corner of her eyes, she had seen the minute hand drift from straight up to straight down. A half hour! Cousin Charlotte was to have been gone but a minute or two! Something dreadful must have happened to the steamer trunk to have kept her away for a whole half hour. And there was still no sign of her anywhere.

Cousin Basil might be arriving at any moment. Would he know Amelia if she were standing there without Cousin

Charlotte? It was certain Amelia would not know *him*! Horses drawing one carriage after another pulled up to the docks. Amelia's heart began to thump every time a single gentleman climbed down from one of those carriages. But every one appeared to find someone waiting for him who was not Amelia.

The hands of the clock moved determinedly on. An hour had now passed, and Amelia's legs were beginning to ache. She was becoming very, very tired. At last, able to stand no longer, she sank down on her portmanteau. There she sat, high-button shoes crossed, hands folded primly on her lap. And waited.

And waited. And waited. And waited.

While at first she was simply uneasy, she rapidly found herself becoming frightened as the arrow that was the minute hand of the remorseless clock moved up again, sharply reminding her that two hours had now passed since Cousin Charlotte had gone off with Mr. Pymm. The passengers from the ship had all left by now, and there was only a handful of dockworkers and ship's crew members remaining on the dock. It was growing colder, and what was worse, darker, for evening was beginning to fall.

Amelia dared not go looking for Cousin Charlotte, for where would she even begin to look? And what if Cousin Charlotte were to return and find her missing? No, she must stay right where she was.

Then, as the hands of the clock moved relentlessly on, and Cousin Charlotte still did not appear, Amelia suddenly remembered Primrose using the words "fed to the sharks." Had Amelia not wondered then if Cousin Charlotte had something like that in mind for her? Was this what the "something" might be, to be abandoned on the docks of a strange city, an orphan left to wander the streets, friendless and penniless, with nothing in her future but a life of beggary, or perhaps worse, to be picked up and given a one-way journey to the workhouse? Oh yes, even petted, pampered Amelia Fairwick knew about *that*! How was it possible that someone would do this to her—no, not just *someone*, but her very own cousin?

Her very own cousin? But was she? Had Primrose not spoken of a play where someone had killed someone else, then pretended to be that person? Murder! Amelia had not even been able to think of such a thing, much less discuss it further with Primrose. Now she could not keep the word out of her head.

Perhaps this person had been *hired* by the real Cousin Charlotte to get rid of the young cousin who would be such a burden in her life. Why else, disliking travel as she did, had this "Cousin Charlotte" come to London to fetch Amelia, only to abandon her on the docks? And was not Amelia, in truth, being abandoned? Could this "Cousin Charlotte" have taken her carpet-bag with her not because she distrusted Amelia, but because she knew she was never coming back? As for the strange Mr. Pymm calling her away, was it not possible that he was her accomplice?

But no, these grim and horrifying thoughts could not be real! Surely, the true Cousin Charlotte would be reappearing at any moment. But she did not. The hands of the clock moved on and on, and still Cousin Charlotte did not come.

"Child, I have seen you sitting here for a very long time. Indeed I have! Are you waiting for someone?"

It took Amelia a moment before she realized that she was being addressed by the little woman who had approached her. Then she quickly jumped up from her portmanteau, and found herself looking into a face round and plump as a ripe apple and just as rosy from the damp, cold air. The owner of the face wore a threadbare, but most respectable, brown woolen coat, and on her head a dowdy brown felt hat had been tugged unceremoniously down over grey hair that crept out in untidy wisps around her face.

"Oh yes!" cried Amelia. "I . . . I . . . " she began, and then could not go on. Hearing a kindly voice after so long had been too much for her.

"There, there, child, it will all come out all right. Indeed it will!" the little woman said. "I shall try to be of help. My name is Mrs. Dobbins. And what is yours, child?"

"A . . . A . . . Amelia Fairwick," replied Amelia, still overcome.

"Well, Amelia," said Mrs. Dobbins, "you must tell me what has happened. Were you expecting someone to come for you?"

"I was with my Cousin Charlotte," Amelia said. "She was called away to see about my steamer trunk but has never returned. It has been . . . it has been . . . " Amelia paused to look over at the clock. "Oh! It has now been very nearly three hours!"

"Three hours!" exclaimed Mrs. Dobbins. "You poor, dear child! I believe I should go at once to speak to an official, and see what I can find out about this. But you must tell me your cousin's last name, dear."

"It's . . . it's . . . " began Amelia, and then stopped in horror. Try as she might, she could not remember Cousin Charlotte's last name.

A curious look crossed Mrs. Dobbins's face. Her eyes widened. "Don't you know it, child?"

So mortified she felt her face flush, Amelia could do little but shake her head.

"Did no one think to tell you?" asked Mrs. Dobbins.

"Yes," replied Amelia. "But I'm afraid I did not pay proper attention." And this was true, for Aunt Felicia *had* given a name when she had first spoken to Amelia of Cousin Charlotte. But Amelia had only noticed miserably that it was not even the same as Mama's had been, and then dismissed it from her mind. And on their long voyage, of course, Cousin Charlotte had always been addressed as "madam."

"Could her name be on her traveling bag?" asked Mrs. Dobbins.

"Cousin Charlotte took it with her," replied Amelia. "This one is mine."

"Oh, dear!" exclaimed Mrs. Dobbins. "But there is someone

standing right over there who is just the one to help us. It is my son. He works here on the docks, and is the very reason I am here, for I bring him his supper whenever he must work evenings. I shall go to him at once. Indeed I shall! Now, you wait right here, as we shouldn't leave your traveling bag unattended, and I fear it would be much too heavy for us to mange. I shall be gone but a moment."

Mrs. Dobbins bustled off, and soon Amelia saw her deep in conference with a young man dressed in the rough clothes of a longshoreman. The two of them approached Amelia.

"This is my son Elmo," said Mrs. Dobbins. "And this, Elmo, is Miss Amelia Fairwick, who has met with such difficulties."

"Ma's told me your story," he began at once. "What I told her's that nearly three hours passing and all, most everyone having doings with the ship coming in, excepting reg'lars like me, well, they've all left. But I'll ask some questions around and about, and see what's to be found out. Do you know where you were to end up? I mean to a hotel, or maybe your cousin's house?"

"I . . . I . . . I was to go to her house. But . . . but I don't know where that is," stammered Amelia, her face burning again.

"And why should you, dear," Mrs. Dobbins broke in quickly. "You were to be with your cousin all the way."

"No matter," said Elmo. "Ma, you'd best take the young miss home with you and give her a bite of supper. I'll be along later after asking some questions around and about. I'll see what I can find out about the lady, and also what's happened with the young miss's steamer trunk."

"There, child," said Mrs. Dobbins. "I told you Elmo would help us. Now you just come along with me. My home is close by. Elmo can bring your traveling bag along with him later, can't you Elmo?"

"No worry, Ma," replied Elmo. With a sudden broad smile, he lifted up Amelia's portmanteau and strode off with it, whistling.

"Now we must go, dear child," said Mrs. Dobbins, taking Amelia cozily by the arm.

But traveling the rough waterfront streets turned out to be anything but a cozy trip for Amelia. She huddled close as she could to Mrs. Dobbins as they passed dark, evil-smelling alleys, small, dingy shops offering what appeared to be less than fresh "fresh goods" and far from fresh fish, decaying brick buildings with rotting boarded-up windows, and threatening stairwells whose stained blackened walls, reeking of mold and mildew, hid secrets too terrible to imagine.

Yet what drove Amelia even closer to the side of Mrs. Dobbins was the bedlam created by people and animals pressing on them from all sides. Snorting horses pulled rickety wagons right up beside them, splashing filthy muddy water onto Amelia's legs. All around them, people shouted and shoved, and were so immune to violent behavior, it appeared, that a horrible street fight between two burly men went almost unnoticed except by a troop of onlooking ruffians cheering them on. Nor was any more attention paid by anyone to the rowdy, unkempt children darting between everyone's legs than to the dirty, ragged bits of paper swirled down the street by the chilling wind.

What if Mrs. Dobbins were not beside her? Amelia asked herself. What if she had had to wander these streets alone, friendless and penniless? Was this not exactly what she had been imagining a short while ago? Of course, she would not, in truth, have been entirely penniless, at least not for awhile. For did she not have twenty-five gold coins, given her by Mr. Collingwood to spend on "frills and fancies," as he phrased it? Frills and fancies! What would Mr. Collingwood think if he had known that those coins might have had to be spent on food and a cot where Amelia could lay her head at night?

But those coins were buried deep in her portmanteau, now in the hands of Elmo Dobbins, whom she had met but a few minutes ago! Yet surely she would have it back again soon. And how could she allow herself to entertain suspicious thoughts of such a kindly young man?

But why was it taking so long to reach their destination? Mrs. Dobbins had said her home was close by. This did not seem "close by" at all. When would they turn into the nice, quiet tree-lined street that would surely be the one where Mrs. Dobbins lived? But they were still on a street that appeared to be as bad as all the others, perhaps worse, and were directly in front of one of the deadly, dark stairwells, when Mrs. Dobbins stopped suddenly.

"Well, dear child," she announced cheerily, "here we are!"

Chapter VIII

A Pitiful Home

Upon hearing Mrs. Dobbins's announcement, Amelia threw her hands to her face, but was unable to hold back a cry of disappointment and dread.

"I am so sorry, child," Mrs. Dobbins said at once. "I know this is not the kind of home you are used to."

"Oh, Mrs. Dobbins, you have been so kind to me. I do thank you with all my heart!" cried Amelia. For wretched as she felt, she could not appear ungrateful for so much kindness.

"Not at all, dear child," replied Mrs. Dobbins, patting Amelia's hand. Then she led the way down the dark, dank steps, and unlocked the door to her home.

And such a pitiful little home it was! They found themselves at first in total darkness, until Mrs. Dobbins struck a match and lit a plain glass oil lamp that sat on a shelf by the door. As the tiny flame flickered upward, it revealed a narrow room with doors to one side that could only lead to unbelievably small rooms, if not to cupboards. At first there was nothing identifiable as windows until Amelia saw two little cavities, one in the front wall and one in the back, both so small it seemed impossible they would ever let in any light at all, and both so high a

52

ladder would be required to look through them.

The furnishings were so few they could be easily taken in at a glance. Four or five faded pictures of country scenes made a brave attempt to hide jagged cracks in the walls. Around a threadbare patch of green carpet sat two skeletal objects, which, on closer look, were seen to be a pine chair and a rocker, parted chip by chip from most of its coat of black paint. A small table and two chairs, equally scarred but otherwise mismatched, stood against the wall. These items, plus a narrow iron cot sitting under the window at the back, were the sum total of the furnishings. It was a sad display indeed.

"Do let me have your coat and bonnet, dear," Mrs. Dobbins said. Taking both from Amelia, she hung them along with her own coat and hat on a row of nails on the wall. "The washroom is through the last door on your right, child. After you have made yourself comfortable, you may wait for me here in the little parlor while I prepare our bit of supper." This said, she lit another glass oil lamp on the small eating table, and bustled off.

A cold stone floor and chipped basin, a far cry from the recent luxury of rose marble and gleaming brass, did not encourage a long visit to the washroom. Amelia returned quickly to perch herself gingerly on the pine chair in the "parlor." Soon she heard the cheerful clink of cups and saucers carried in on a tin tray together with a teapot, the tiniest of milk pitchers and sugar bowls, and a dish of edibles, brought in by Mrs. Dobbins from her kitchen. Seated at the table, Amelia was served at once with "a nice hot cup of tea" with buttered bread and a "nice slice of cold beef."

"Now, dear, you must take all the sugar you want," said Mrs. Dobbins, seeing Amelia help herself politely to the smallest teaspoonful imaginable. "Children do so love their sugar in a cup of tea. Indeed they do!"

"Oh, thank you, Mrs. Dobbins," said Amelia, helping herself to a tiny bit more.

"Tsk, tsk, dear child," said Mrs. Dobbins, "there must be no more 'Mrs. Dobbins.' Children I used to care for always called me *Nanny* Dobbins, and it would please me ever so much if you would do so too."

"I will if you wish it, N . . . N . . . Nanny Dobbins," replied Amelia, faltering from shyness.

"There, that's much better," Mrs. Dobbins said. "And now that that's settled, you must tell me all about yourself."

And so, to the sounds of a radiator gurgling softly against the wall, and the gentle flickering light of the oil lamps, Amelia began to tell "all about herself." Oh, not quite "all," for she still could not bring herself to tell of her terrible suspicions about Cousin Charlotte. Nor, in truth, could she even tell of Primrose, because after all, meeting with her against Cousin Charlotte's wishes had no doubt been a wicked, wicked thing to do.

But she did tell about how she had lost sweet Mama when she was but a baby, and most recently beloved Papa, thus making her an orphan. She went on to speak of Polly, and Aunt Felicia, and all her special friends at Mrs. Draper's Academy. She even told Mrs. Dobbins of the most special possessions she had brought with her in her portmanteau—her doll Gwendolyn, her favorite books, and the reticule she was embroidering for Aunt Felicia. And finally, hesitating but a moment, she told of the gold coins, which, she said, she wished to share with Mrs. Dobbins to repay the kindness shown her. Needless to say, Mrs. Dobbins retorted most indignantly that she would accept no such thing. Indeed she would not!

At last it did seem to Amelia that it must be getting very late. As much as she had enjoyed her supper and the comforting talk with Mrs. Dobbins, she was very tired. Where was Elmo Dobbins? Should he not have been there by now with her portmanteau at the very least, if not with news of Cousin Charlotte?

Mrs. Dobbins must have had the very same thought for she pulled a watch, the plainest of plain nickel-plated variety, from the pocket of her grey muslin dress. "Oh my goodness!" she exclaimed. "Where is that boy of mine? Oh, dear child, how tired you must be!" she said, for she had seen Amelia trying to stifle a yawn. "You poor dear, we must put you to bed at once. You shall have my room, and I shall wait up here for Elmo, to receive his news."

"Oh, I could not take your room, Nanny Dobbins!" cried Amelia. "Where will you sleep then?"

"Why, in the cot out here, of course," said Mrs. Dobbins quite matter-of-factly. "Now there's to be no more nonsense about it, child. Off you go."

Too weary to resist further, it was but a short time later that Amelia, her petticoat serving as a nightdress, was climbing into the cot in the small room that served as Mrs. Dobbins's bedroom. On a chair beside the bed, Amelia's pale-blue woolen dress with the cutwork linen collar lay neatly folded. Until her portmanteau was delivered, she would have to wear that same dress, even though Mrs. Dobbins shook her head over the spots of mud that had splashed up on the skirt, as well as on her coat, during their journey from the docks.

"We must see to those!" she said. "But morning will be time enough for that. For now, good night, child!"

"Good night, Nanny Dobbins," said Amelia.

"Dear, dear child!" murmured Mrs. Dobbins as she softly shut the door.

But the door had no sooner closed behind her than Amelia's eyes, heavy though they had become, flew wide open. Thrust so suddenly into the deep darkness of the tiny musty room, she felt as frightened as she had on that first terrible night in her cabin aboard the ship. Even more! For now there were questions spinning around in her head, questions with no answers, or with answers so terrifying she could hardly bear to think about them. Spinning! Spinning! Oh, if only they would stop! After all, she must remember that she was no longer quite as alone as she had been. She now had Mrs. Dobbins. No, *Nanny* Dobbins, who would try to help her.

It was a comforting thought, and it finally served its purpose. The spinning became slower. And slower. Until sleep closed Amelia's heavy eyes, and at long last, the spinning stopped altogether.

Chapter IX

Why?

W hen next her eyes opened, Amelia was looking at a tiny slice of window high up in the bedroom wall. It was letting in the cold grey light of morning. Once again, she could not remember where she was. Why was her bed not rocking like a giant cradle as it had for so many days? And where was the sound of rushing water and the now familiar creak-creaking of the walls around her? From somewhere outside the window came the distant clop-clop of horses' hooves. Inside the room, still in near darkness, there was only an odd musty smell and dead silence— nothing to remind her of where she was. But all at once, into her head jumped the picture of a round face with apple-pink cheeks, grey hair, and kind grey eyes. Mrs. Dobbins! And she was, of course, in Mrs. Dobbins's room!

Mrs. Dobbins, who might long since have been up. Mrs. Dobbins, who more than likely was in possession of news of Cousin Charlotte from Elmo Dobbins, not to mention Amelia's portmanteau with its precious contents. She quickly threw back her cover and climbed from the cot, shivering with cold and fearful expectation as she stood on the icy floor, reaching for her dress lying folded on the chair. She lifted it up, but before she even started to unfold it, she let out a startled gasp. This was not her dress at all!

Could she be mistaken? It hardly seemed so, for this dress was the roughest kind of cotton, while hers had been of the softest cashmere wool. And even in the dim light, she could see that the dress was much darker than hers of pale sky blue. She let the dress unfold all the way and held it up closer to the little bit of light coming through the window. It was, in truth, the plainest, shabbiest, drabbest, *ugliest* dress she had ever seen, looking more like a potato sack than a dress.

Amelia fought back tears. Why would Mrs. Dobbins have wanted to play such a curious and cruel joke on her? It must have been Mrs. Dobbins who had done this. Who else was there? No one, of course. And yet suddenly, tears turned to suppressed laughter as Amelia realized her own dimwittedness. It must have been Mrs. Dobbins who had replaced the dress, but not as a joke. It was for the very best of reasons! Had she not spoken of the mud spots on Amelia's dress? Dear Nanny Dobbins, thought Amelia. She could not bear waiting to clean it, so had found Amelia a substitute dress while this was being done. How she had managed it on such short notice, it was impossible to guess. But Amelia knew she should put it on and not reveal for a moment how ugly she thought it was.

She was dismayed to discover that she must also hide how she felt about the ugly shoes and rough stockings that had replaced her soft kidskin high-button shoes and fine-combed cotton stockings, undoubtedly replaced for the same reason as the dress. But she was determined to say nothing about these either.

Finding no one in the "parlor" after she had dressed, Amelia made a hasty trip to the washroom, only to find the room still deserted when she returned. The cot where Mrs. Dobbins was to have slept was neatly made up, looking just as it had the night before. And though heavy boots thumping on the pavement, horses' hooves clattering, and the loud voices of a noisy street could be heard from outside the front window, all inside was remarkably quiet. Deadly quiet. Amelia ran to peer into the kitchen, a room no larger than the tiny washroom she had just left, only to discover that Mrs. Dobbins was not there either. Where then? Where could she have gone?

Amelia then noticed something else—her portmanteau was nowhere to be seen. Oh yes, that was it! Of course! Elmo Dobbins must have never arrived, and Mrs. Dobbins had gone to find him. Soon she would be there accompanied by both her son and the portmanteau. Amelia sat down on the "parlor" chair, certain that they would be arriving at any moment.

But moments passed, and then minutes. Did an hour go by? With no clock in the room, Amelia had no idea, but at long last she heard a key grating in the front door. This must surely be Mrs. Dobbins! With a joyful cry, Amelia jumped from the chair and ran to the door. It swung open, and she came to a sudden, horrified stop.

In the doorway stood a large, heavyset woman in a garish black-and-white checkered coat. A shapeless black felt hat, filthy with grease and other stains, was jammed like a pancake on her head over straggly hair of no nameable color, and certainly no cleaner than the hat that attempted to cover it. In one arm the woman clutched a parcel wrapped in newspaper and tied with a dirty string.

But Amelia barely saw all this. Her eyes were held by another pair of eyes, tiny and sharp as a weasel's, squinting at her from a wide, flat face that sat under the hat like a great blotched plate. A spreading nose, covered with a network of blue veins, which bespoke its owner's particular interest in liquid refreshments, formed its centerpiece. There was in truth enough that was dreadful about the face that a large ugly mole set prominently on the chin hardly seemed to matter.

What did matter, however, was that unless Amelia was in the

middle of the worst nightmare of her life, there was no way in the whole world that this person could be mistaken for Mrs. Dobbins.

"Well," said the woman, "pop your eyes back in your head, dearie!"

"But I expected . . . I expected . . . " stammered Amelia. "I . . . I thought you were Mrs. Dobbins."

"Huh!" snorted the woman. "Not now and never was. I'm Mrs. Shrike, for your information. And now if you'll kindly step aside, I'd like to drop this stuff down someplace. Here, this is the place," she said, and went stumping into the kitchen. When she banged her parcel down, the distinct clank of bottles knocking together could be clearly heard.

"But where *is* Mrs. Dobbins?" Amelia asked when Mrs. Shrike reappeared through the kitchen door.

"How should I know? All I know is she ain't here," snapped Mrs. Shrike, grunting as she peeled off her checkered coat. "Ooops! Almost forgot!" She pulled a key from the pocket, shoved it into the lock on the front door, and gave it a fierce twist. Then she turned to Amelia with a sly grin, displaying two gaping holes in what might otherwise have been a perfect row of crooked blackened teeth. "Wouldn't want any of this valuable stuff around here to get stolen, now would we, dearie?"

Amelia had no idea whether reference was being made to the bottles just deposited in the kitchen or the furnishings displayed around them in the parlor, but she felt the safest thing to do was simply shake her head. Mrs. Shrike did not appear to be someone it would be wise to offend. Now somewhat over her first shock, Amelia began to wonder who Mrs. Shrike was. Could she be a friend of Mrs. Dobbins, asked to stay until she returned? Mrs. Shrike seemed an unlikely kind of friend for Mrs. Dobbins to have, but there were some things, Amelia knew, for which there was simply no accounting.

Her eyes followed Mrs. Shrike as she stumped over to hang

her coat and hat on the wall, now noticing for the first time that Mrs. Dobbins's hat and coat were missing from the row of nails. And so was something else—Amelia's own coat and bonnet! Oh, a coat was there, all right, but it must have come from the same source as her dress, being equally shapeless, shabby, and ugly. Amelia could understand why Mrs. Dobbins might have taken her coat to be cleaned as well as the dress, but for the missing bonnet there could be no explanation.

So far, Amelia had been able to invent explanations for almost everything, but explanations were becoming increasingly difficult to come by. Mrs. Dobbins was the only person who could supply them, but where was she? Amelia finally found the courage to ask.

"Mrs. Shrike, did . . . did Mrs. Dobbins say when she might return?"

"Not to me she didn't," said Mrs. Shrike, scowling as she leaned over to pick up her coat, which she was having some difficulty in hanging up on the nail.

Amelia hesitated. "Did . . . did she go for my portmanteau?"

"Your port . . . man . . . *what?*" asked Mrs. Shrike.

"My traveling bag," explained Amelia.

Mrs. Shrike lifted one eyebrow significantly. "Did it have valuables in it?"

"I . . . don't . . . " faltered Amelia, caught by surprise. She did not think this was something she should reveal to Mrs. Shrike.

"Of course you do, dearie," said Mrs. Shrike shrewdly. Then she snickered. "Never mind that dress you're in. I can tell what I can tell, and I suspect you have enough in your port . . . man . . . toe to buy and sell everything here one thousand times over. You'd better not expect to see it again . . . your Mrs. Dobbins neither, if you know what smart is. Now, I'll go see if there's something for you to eat." With that, she went thumping back into the kitchen.

Amelia stood staring after her, feeling as if her heart had turned to stone. Betrayed by yet another person! And who could have believed it of apple-cheeked, grey-haired, kind-eyed Mrs. Dobbins? No, not Mrs. Dobbins—"Nanny" Dobbins! Oh! Oh! Oh! How could Amelia have been so taken in? Sitting there cozily telling all about the twenty-five gold coins, and thinking how later she would insist upon Mrs. Dobbins taking one no matter how much she objected to it. And all along, Mrs. Dobbins was thinking—*knowing*—that she would soon be the owner of all twenty-five!

Amelia had a moment of relief in remembering that she had not spoken of the other valuable treasures in her portmanteau: her gold pocket watch, the brooch, and the bracelet set with diamonds and true pearls, which had belonged to Mama. Mrs. Dobbins did not know of those. Did not know? Oh, what a joke that was! Of course she knew, as soon as she went off to join Elmo Dobbins, who no doubt knew of every last item. Why, they were nothing but a pair of very clever thieves! Clever thieves who had even stolen her clothes, to sell without doubt, for it was certain they must know the value of everything. And here was yet another joke, her thinking kind Mrs. Dobbins had taken them to be cleaned. *Kind* Mrs. Dobbins, who had given up her room to Amelia—yes, so she could more easily creep out when Amelia was asleep.

But who was Mrs. Shrike? How was she connected to Mrs. Dobbins? Was she a thief as well or just somebody hired by Mrs. Dobbins to guard Amelia, perhaps in return for a bottle or two of her favorite refreshments? And if so, why? Why not just let Amelia go? But for some reason, she was not to be let go. Oh yes, she had seen that door being locked!

"This here's your porridge," announced Mrs. Shrike, arriving from the kitchen, breathing out powerful fumes of whatever she had without doubt been sampling from one of her bottles. In her hands she carried a bowl filled with something that so resembled grey cement it was small wonder a spoon was able to stand straight up in it as if it were a sentry guarding the contents.

Mrs. Shrike flung the bowl down on the table. "You can eat it or not, dearie, but it's what you're getting, and no more where it comes from until I get back, whenever that is." With that, she threw on her coat, jammed her hat on her head, and stumped out the front door. The key grated in the lock, and then the door was tested to make certain the key had done its work. If there had been any doubt before, there was none now. Amelia was a prisoner!

But still the grim question remained, Why?

Chapter X

The Only Chance

Amelia felt that day would never end as she wandered aimlessly in her lonely underground cell, for so it could rightly be called. Her only companions were the indifferent boots and shoes passing by the window high up in the front wall, a horrifying large brown rat scurrying to his secret lair in the kitchen, and Mrs. Shrike, who indeed did return as she had said she would.

It was nearing nightfall, however, before she arrived, bearing an unwrapped loaf of bread under her arm. With this encumbrance, she still managed to lock the door before stumping across the room to throw the loaf down on the table, along with a small newspaper-wrapped packet, which she pulled from her pocket. After lighting the two oil lamps, she rushed into the kitchen without bothering to remove her coat and hat. A few minutes later she emerged, reeking of the same fumes that had accompanied her on her earlier visit there. The trip to the kitchen seemed to have cheered her immeasurably.

"I see you ate all your nice porridge," she said, finally acknowledging Amelia's presence with something better than the grunt she had delivered on her arrival.

"Yes, thank you," said Amelia, who in truth had been able to choke down but two horrible sticky teaspoonfuls before removing the bowl to the kitchen. It appeared that the rat had enjoyed all the "nice" porridge, but Amelia hardly dared suggest it.

"Well, enjoy your supper, dearie," said Mrs. Shrike, lumbering a trifle unsteadily out the front door, although not so far cheered by her visit that she forgot to turn the key in the lock behind her. No indeed, she would never forget *that!*

As soon as the sound of her heavy footsteps had disappeared up the outside stairs, Amelia sat down at the table to confront her supper. The loaf of bread did not appear to be too clean, and Amelia soon discovered, upon tasting it, that it must have left the baker's oven days earlier. Yet even so, it was an improvement over the porridge, and she was able to eat some of it. The contents of the newspaper packet, however, turned out to be a lump of extraordinarily unpleasant-smelling grease, something she could hardly bear to look at, much less taste.

Porridge! Bread! Grease! Was this not the very menu described to a horrified Amelia not so very long ago? This, the selfsame Amelia who had not marveled at a hot muffin dripping with butter and honey, a cup of sweet milk, and a plump red apple being served to her right in the middle of a vast ocean. Now she could really know why an apple had meant so much to Primrose. Now she could know how it felt to long for one herself!

A small scratching sound made its way down one side of the bedroom floor, then it stopped. A moment later it started up again. Stop. Start. Stop. Was it the rat? Would he climb into the cot? Amelia quickly drew up her knees to bring her toes away from the foot of the cot, and lay there barely breathing, stiff with fright. A moment passed. Another one. Then at last the scratching started up again, and continued out the door. Amelia jumped up from the cot, flew to the door, and slammed it shut. Then she flew back to bed, where she lay trembling. As it was, she had been tossing in her cot for what seemed like hours. How would she ever be able to fall asleep now?

She heard a woman's sharp shriek of laughter cutting through the night, followed by a man's rough, angry shout, and from somewhere else the mournful sound of a baby wailing. All these were fearful enough when heard in broad daylight, but how much worse they seemed when they found their way into the suffocating darkness and silence of a room buried in the ground. Even the clop-clop of horses' hooves became a sinister and threatening sound. Amelia pulled her pillow around her ears to try to drown them out. But she could no more do that than stop her dread of the rat finding another way to creep back into her room—or stop the questions twisting and turning in her head.

Why was she being held prisoner? Was it for something she still owned? But what did she have left that thieves might want? It could not be her locket, for who knew about it? Hidden behind her dress from the time she left the ship, the locket had not been mentioned to Mrs. Dobbins. Even when she climbed into bed the night before, it had been hidden behind her petticoat, safe from prying eyes.

But if the answer did not lie in the locket, what then? And when would she find out? How many more nights must she spend like this one? How many more days like the one just past? How much longer must she wonder what was to become of her? Could it be tomorrow that someone would come through the door and tell her?

Two more days and nights passed, however, and still no one came to the door but Mrs. Shrike. Her visits took place at any time that it pleased her to come, although this mattered little to Amelia. Nor did it matter to her when Mrs. Shrike announced that she was "not up to cooking," for Amelia was in truth not up to *eating* anything Mrs. Shrike cooked, if the porridge was any sample. Of Mrs. Shrike's two offerings, Amelia preferred the stale bread. The rat got the grease.

What did matter to her was that Mrs. Shrike never had much to say. Oh, Amelia did not really want any cozy conversations with her, but did want to find out if she knew more than she had let on at the beginning. Her visits, however, although they always included a trip to the kitchen, were remarkably short. And after saying what she had to say, she otherwise did little more than grunt. How could Amelia ask questions of such a person?

But when the third murderous night finally ended, Amelia determined that she would make herself ask. As soon as Mrs. Shrike came through the door, Amelia would say, "Why am I being held prisoner?" Yes, that is exactly what she would do! And although her courage slipped several times, she was ready when she finally heard someone struggling to insert the key in the lock, and Mrs. Shrike walked in.

No, wobbled in was more like it. Her face puffed and redder than ever, her hat so askew it looked in imminent danger of falling off her head, she lurched across the floor to the table and fell into a chair with a monumental thud. Then she flung her arms across the table and, with a deep sigh, let her head fall between them. Her eyelids drooped shut, her jaw fell slack, and in moments the sounds of her great thundering snores were rumbling around the room. She was clearly unable to accept questions, so Amelia would have to wait.

Mrs. Shrike had also clearly forgotten to bring Amelia anything to eat, for she had brought nothing with her, not the usual loaf of bread—not anything. Amelia already knew that the one tiny cupboard in the kitchen was empty, but she went in to fetch the remainder of yesterday's loaf, which she had left on the sink. And she discovered that someone had been there before her. Only a small part of the loaf was left, the rest gnawed away by the rat. With a shudder, Amelia flew from the kitchen and sank into the rocking chair, trying to forget what she had just seen as she waited for Mrs. Shrike to awaken.

While Amelia rocked and waited, Mrs. Shrike snored on, for

all the world *dead* to the world. She would probably not so much as twitch if someone were to remove the key from her pocket, unlock the door, and run off. Amelia, however, had never given a moment's thought to the idea of trying to escape. After all, was it not better to stay with the known horror than face the unknown, and possibly far worse one, beyond the door?

And if she did escape, what would she do—a young girl barely turned eleven, adrift in the streets of a giant city, so foreign to her and so frightening? Besides, where would she run? To Cousin Charlotte, who had deserted her on the docks? To Cousin Basil, who had never even bothered to come for her, or shown in any way that he wanted her at all? *If* she could find them, that is. No, better to stay where she was and hope that, like all her fairy tales, somehow everything would end happily ever after.

Anyway, even if she had entertained the notions of escaping, and decided to do it now, it would mean dipping her hand into Mrs. Shrike's coat pocket for the key. All danger aside, it made her skin creep just to think of it. No, she could never do such a thing! Which of course ended all possible ideas of escape, for one thing Mrs. Shrike had never failed to do was to lock the door when she left and when she entered. *Never!*

Never? Amelia's rocking chair came to a sudden stop. Had Mrs. Shrike not done so *this* time? Had she not simply come through the door, very nearly toppled over as she bumped the door shut with her shoulder, and then gone stumbling across the floor to the table? Amelia jumped from the rocker and ran to the door. Twisting the handle slowly and noiselessly, she pulled gently on the door. It came right toward her! She drew in her breath sharply, and then quickly closed the door again. This was all too unexpected and too startling—the opportunity to run off right before her, without any key needed.

But was it what she wanted to do? Why would escaping be any less dangerous or foolish now than it had been but a few moments ago? Had anything changed, other than the discovery that the door was now known to be unlocked? It would all be different if she knew anyone in the city besides her strange and forbidding cousins or where they might be if she chose to go to them. But she knew no one. No one except Primrose.

Primrose! Oh, would it not be wonderful if she could find Primrose? Yes, but of what help could Primrose be to her, another young girl no older than she was? Well, Primrose was so full of story ideas, might she not be able to think of one that could be helpful? Further, did not Mr. Smeech and Mr. Turk appear to want Primrose to speak with Amelia on the docks?

But how could Primrose be found any more than Cousin Charlotte or Cousin Basil? All Amelia knew was that Primrose was to be at a theatre. *What* theatre? There must be dozens in such a big city. Primrose had told Amelia the name of it, but all she could remember was Primrose saying it was "punier" than it sounded. And it *did* sound like something grand and royal, Amelia remembered thinking then. Something grand and royal. Might that be a palace? Or a castle? Castle! That was it! And surely if one knew the name, any theatre could be found. All one had to do was ask.

But Amelia had no sooner come up with the solutions to the problems of escaping than her resolution to do so collapsed. What was she thinking, embarking on such a venture? What if none of the things worked out as she had imagined they would? What would she do then? No, she had better stay where she was after all.

But stay with rats gnawing at her food? Stay with Mrs. Shrike as her only human companion? Stay to face nights spent curled up in terror lest a rat should crawl into her bed? Stay to face deadly days that gave no promise of any fairy-tale happy ending? And was it not possible that what was happening to her was of such a sinister and foreboding nature, something far more terrible than wandering the streets might be in store for her? And might not this be her only chance to do anything about it?

Swiftly she tiptoed back past the rocking chair and the loudly snoring Mrs. Shrike to where the shabby coat hung on the wall. Carefully she took it down and crept with it back to the door. Then silent as a shadow, she opened the door and slipped out. Her heart was pounding so hard she could hardly draw a breath as she stood outside the closed door, but no matter what, she was *not* going back through it again.

Chapter XI

A Homeless Orphan

No sooner had Amelia started down the street than she came perilously close to turning and rushing right back to the safe haven of her prison. For although she thought she had known what it felt like to be alone, she realized almost at once that there had always been someone, no matter how unpleasant, watching over her, be it the cold, unfeeling Cousin Charlotte, the thieving, lying Mrs. Dobbins, or the dreadful Mrs. Shrike. Now she was but a homeless orphan, clothed in what might truly be called "rags," wandering the streets of New York alone. Though she had been thoroughly shaken by all that went on around her when she huddled beside Mrs. Dobbins on her first journey through the city streets, it was nothing compared to the fear she felt now.

How much more threatening everything suddenly became with no one by her side—the carriages and vans rumbling by, the horses stomping and snorting clouds of steam into the air, the dogs barking, the tradesmen shouting and arguing with one another in loud, angry voices.

"Hey, can't you watch where you're going, missy?" a rough voice barked at her. It seemed to come from nowhere.

Totally bewildered by all the noise and the clatter, Amelia had not heard the cart being wheeled up toward the doors of a dingy storefront she was passing. Trying to escape it, she stumbled and fell to her knees. Her eyes stung with tears as she quickly scrambled to her feet, for her hands were scraped and her knees ached. The man had already disappeared into the store with his cart, and people streaming past seemed to look right through her as if she were not even there. She had become as invisible as any sodden leaf lying in the gutter. Oh yes, she was indeed alone and on her own! Yet, she had determined not to go back, and she would not change her mind over a little tumble to the sidewalk. She would *not*!

But how her knees did ache, and oh, how very cold she was. The icy wind bit so deeply into her bones she felt as if they would snap like icicles. And why had her bonnet been taken from her and not even replaced? She put her frozen fingers up over her ears to protect them from the wind, but that did no good at all. She finally gave up and thrust her hands into her pockets, and then made a discovery. One of the pockets had buried deep inside it, a scarf!

It was only an ugly brown cotton scarf, not even warm wool, but Amelia felt as if she had come upon buried treasure. She turned to the shop window beside her and, using it as a mirror, threw the scarf over her head and tied it under her chin. When she saw her reflection, she was not certain whether to laugh or cry, for the Amelia Fairwick she had known all her life had disappeared. In her place stood a street urchin with torn stockings, a shabby coat, ugly boots, and what was nothing better than a kerchief over her head. Even Papa would not have recognized this little girl! But at least now her ears felt warmer and her hands could be kept in her pockets.

So far, however, although she had put several blocks between herself and the prison she had left, she had yet to find the courage to approach a stranger and ask the way to the Castle Theatre. But at last she arrived at a part of the city that appeared to be less rough than the one she had left. There she came upon a pleasant-looking woman standing and gazing at an array of hats in a shop window.

Amelia took a hesitant step toward her. "Excuse me, please," she said timidly.

The look on the woman's face instantly turned cold and suspicious. Her fingers tightened around her purse, as if she thought Amelia was preparing to rob her.

"Could . . . could you tell me, please, where the Castle Theatre is?" Amelia asked.

"No, I can't," snapped the woman. "I've never heard of it." With that, she rushed into the hat store, only looking back, it appeared, to make certain Amelia was not following her.

This cruel encounter caused Amelia to be even more timid when she approached the next person, an elderly gentleman. He did at least speak to her kindly, but no, he too had never heard of the Castle Theatre. Perhaps the policeman on the corner could help her, the gentleman suggested.

"Oh, thank you!" said Amelia, but did not tell him that she hardly dared ask a policeman anything. For might not a policeman ask questions as well as give answers—questions that could end up in a trip to the workhouse? No, Amelia could not risk that.

Trudging up one street and down another, buffeted by the hordes of people on the sidewalk, growing colder and more weary with every step, she did at last find a young man who knew of the Castle Theatre, and could tell her where to find it. But what a long way away it still was! Several times she was certain she had lost her way, and had to find the courage to ask for help from yet another stranger.

There were times when she wondered if she was getting any closer to the theatre or simply getting farther and farther away from it. Daylight had begun to fade, and the gaslights that lined the streets were already beginning to cast their eerie glow upon the street scenes below. What would she do if she had still not found the theatre when night fell? Would she have to huddle in some doorway, and perhaps have some nameless, faceless "shape" huddling in the doorway with her? Hunching up her shoulders and digging her hands more deeply into her pockets, Amelia shuddered.

On and on she trudged, past one building after another. Finally, she began to pass some theatres, but they were large, important-looking buildings like the one Papa had taken her to in London. Surely the Castle Theatre could not be among them. Yet this is where she had been told to come, so she must keep on looking.

If only her feet were not so sore or her legs so tired. But she must go on. She must! At last, however, she could no longer drag one foot after the other, so she sank down on a stone step to rest. It would be but for a moment, she thought.

Across from her stood a row of old nondescript buildings distinguished only by the crooked shutters that hung tipsily from a few of their dusty windows. And if their brick walls had ever possessed any nameable color, it had long been hidden under layers of soot and city grime. There was surely nothing here that could begin to pass for a theatre. Amelia had missed seeing the street sign at the corner and was certain she had taken yet another wrong turn. This dingy, shadowy street was not a place she cared to linger, and after a few minutes, hurriedly jumped up to leave. Yet she had taken but a step or two when her eyes were riveted to something curious happening directly across the street.

Tiny pinpoints of light suddenly appeared over a double doorway that she had taken to be the entrance to a coach house. A moment passed, and then the lights flared up into little blue and yellow flames that flickered around a marquee jutting narrowly out over the sidewalk. The lights picked out glints of gold from letters strung out across the marquee—the letters read CASTLE THEATRE.

Castle Theatre! It was all so quick, so startling, that at first Amelia barely noticed the young boy carrying a large broom emerge from the dark passageway beside the building and start sweeping the sidewalk under the marquee. But then her hopes rose. Was this not someone who could help her find Primrose? Heart beating wildly, and fast as her clumpy boots could carry her, Amelia went flying across the street.

Chapter XII

A Startling Revelation

The boy in front of the theatre looked up when he heard Amelia's footsteps, but he paid no further attention and went right on with his sweeping. Amelia found herself addressing the tousled brown hair falling over his forehead.

"E . . . e . . . excuse me, please," she faltered. "But could you tell me where I might find Miss Primrose Lagoon?"

The boy's broom stopped in midair. "Who is it wants to know?" he asked, looking at her sharply.

"M . . . me," said Amelia.

"Don't you have a name?" asked the boy.

"It's Amelia. Amelia Fairwick." And then, feeling somehow that the boy might expect to hear more, Amelia added, "I met Primrose when we were on the ship coming from London."

The boy's face registered nothing throughout this explanation. When it had ended, he said abruptly, "Wait here. I'll go get her."

His broom perched jauntily over his shoulders, he disappeared into the narrow passageway from which he had just appeared. But he had no sooner left than his head popped back out around the corner, and he beckoned to Amelia. "You better come with me."

Amelia scurried after him through the dark, malodorous passageway as he made his way toward a battered black door with one lamp flickering palely above it. The boy cautiously opened the door, peering in as if he were afraid of who might be behind it. He then beckoned again to Amelia, and they both slipped into a dimly lit corridor lined with some six or seven doors, each a different color, and all sadly in want of paint. The boy led Amelia to one of the doors, the one that was a dingy dark grey, and opened it.

"Wait here," he said. "Stay in here, and don't open the door. I'll go fetch Primrose." Then he hurriedly left, closing the door behind himself with a firm click.

What a strange reception room this was! A single lamp cast its fluttering light over an assortment of brooms, mops, buckets, and several rags hanging from pegs on the wall. Unless two upturned buckets could be considered as such, the room offered no chairs at all. In truth it gave every indication of being no more than a broom closet. Unless the boy felt that Amelia's appearance did not warrant his putting her in a respectable waiting room, she might almost think that he was hiding her!

Being enclosed in such a small room with nothing to do but stare at mops, brooms, and rags made Amelia feel that her wait was a long one. But perhaps it might have been no more than five min utes before she saw the handle turn, the door open a crack, and finally open just enough to allow someone to slip in and quickly close the door. That someone was dressed in a pink velveteen dress with billowing petticoats, and golden curls floated out over her shoulders. It was, of course, Primrose! But instead of smiling, she only tilted her head and studied Amelia with a puzzled frown.

"Would you please take that rag off your head?" she demanded.

Amelia's hesitant smile faded as she pulled off her scarf and stuffed it into her coat pocket. Why was her friend Primrose behaving in such an odd, unfriendly way?

But then Primrose grinned. It was the same mischievous grin Amelia remembered. "Creepers!" Primrose said. "It really is you,

Amelia. I wasn't certain it was you even if that is the name you gave."

Amelia now remembered her reflection in the shop window. She could not help giggling. "I guess I wouldn't have known me either."

"What kind of costume is that you have on, anyway?" Primrose asked. "I don't mean to injure your feelings, but you look awful, Amelia."

"I know," Amelia said. "My clothes were all stolen."

"Didn't you have anything else to put on?" Primrose asked. "You had lots of other clothes, didn't you?"

"Yes, but everything else was stolen, too," replied Amelia.

"Well, you ought to do something about it as soon as you can," said Primrose. "Now, if you'll care to give me your coat, I'll hang it up."

But when Amelia peeled off her coat, Primrose could only look at the dress under it and shake her head in disbelief. "As soon as you can, Amelia," she repeated sternly. It did not seem to matter at all to her that her own dress was worn, faded, and more than a little in need of repairs.

Before hanging Amelia's coat up, however, Primrose cracked open the door once more and peeked out. "Washroom's next door, case you're interested. The coast is clear, but check before you come back. Don't want anyone knowing you're here, not yet anyway."

By the time Amelia had safely returned, Primrose was already seated comfortably atop one of the overturned buckets. "You haven't said what you're doing here," she said as Amelia lowered herself precariously onto the second bucket.

"I ran away," Amelia said simply. "I . . . I didn't have any place else to go, Primrose."

"You mean you left your creeping Cousin Charlotte?" Primrose shuddered. "Can't say I blame you."

"No, I didn't run away from *her*," Amelia explained. "She left me waiting for her at the docks and never came back."

"I said there was something fishy about her, didn't I?" said Primrose proudly. "Anyway, what about the other cousin . . . your Cousin Basil? Wasn't that his name? Is *he* the one you ran away from?"

Amelia shook her head. "No. He never came at all!"

Primrose rolled up her eyes and stared at the ceiling, clearly trying to determine what she could make of this new piece of information. In the end, she gave a deep and hopeless sigh. "I guess I can't think of any stories I ever heard to explain this. Anyway, it's been four days since the ship got here from London, Amelia. You weren't sitting on the docks for four days waiting for someone to come get you, were you?"

"No," replied Amelia, a trifle indignantly, although in truth she could not entirely blame Primrose for considering this possibility. "A kind lady named Mrs. Dobbins . . . well, I *thought* she was kind . . . was bringing supper to her son, Elmo Dobbins. She found me sitting all by myself on the dock, and she invited me to where she lives. It wasn't a very nice place though. It was in a cellar, and there were even rats. And, Primrose, Mrs. Dobbins and Elmo turned out to be thieves! They stole all my clothes and my portmanteau. It . . . it had twenty-five gold coins in it, and Mama's jewels, and everything."

"Creepers!" exclaimed Primrose. "So *they're* the ones you ran away from."

"N . . . not exactly," said Amelia. "I ran away from a dreadful person named Mrs. Shrike. She came after Mrs. Dobbins disappeared."

"Wheeoo!" Primrose whistled. "In all my born days I never heard such a mixed-up story. But how did you escape from this Mrs. Shrike then?"

"She forgot to lock the door this morning, and fell asleep on the table," replied Amelia. "But I don't even know why I was locked up at all. I didn't have anything else for Mrs. Dobbins to steal. I mean, except for my locket, which she didn't know about."

"Hmmmmph!" Primrose tightened her lips. "I don't know about some things, but I know a lot about villains and kidnapping and things like that, Amelia. What I think is that you were locked up because you were being held for ransom."

"Ransom!" cried Amelia. "But who would pay ransom for me?"

"Your Cousin Charlotte or Cousin Basil might," replied Primrose, raising her eyebrows knowingly. "Or at least that's what Mrs. Dobbins and her son might think. There you are standing all alone on the dock looking rich as can be, and along they came and nipped you up. Now they're off looking for your Cousins C. and B., and leaving you in the care of Mrs. Shrike."

"But ... but I didn't ... I didn't know ... " stammered Amelia, her face grown hot with embarrassment over the confession she must make. "I didn't know their names or where they lived. I ... I don't know now."

Primrose only shrugged indifferently. "Not surprising, all things considered. Anyway, I figured you would have gone there instead of coming here, if you had known where *there* was."

"But if I didn't tell Mrs. Dobbins, how would she know?" asked Amelia.

"Easy enough. If Elmo Dobbins works on the docks, he's got ways," Primrose said. She shifted uncomfortably. "I ... I think even Smeech and Turk know."

Amelia very nearly toppled off her bucket. "How?"

"Oh," said Primrose with a sigh, "I was creeping stupid enough to tell them about you on the ship. They figured some day, you being so rich, it might come in handy if I was to stay friends with you. They're always looking out for stuff like that, those two. I don't know how they found out anything. Maybe they got into the hold and looked up your trunk, if you had one. Maybe they bribed someone on the ship. I just think they know, that's all."

"Should I ask them?" said Amelia.

"Not in a million creeping years!" said Primrose. "If they found out they had you in their hands, *they'd* be the ones turning you in for ransom, more than likely. Why do you think we're sitting in here instead of someplace better, Amelia? We're hiding from Smeech and Turk, that's why!"

"But it was the boy who brought me in here," said Amelia. "Why did *he* do that?"

"Oh, I told him about you," replied Primrose. "It's all right. He won't say anything."

"Well, if you don't think I should ask Mr. Smeech or Mr. Turk how to find Cousin Basil, would you ask them for me?" said Amelia.

"They'd smell a mouse if I asked them," replied Primrose. "Anyway, I don't think you ought to go finding your Cousin Basil until you find out why he didn't come finding you. Something's creeping funny about it all."

"But what am I to do?" Amelia asked in despair. "I haven't anyplace else to go, and I can't live here in a closet."

Primrose remained silent for a few moments. "I do have an idea," she said at last. "But I have to go now, because they'll all be coming into the theatre soon, and I have to do my performance. You'll be safe here, though you mustn't open the door, not even a crack. I'm sorry it will be such a long wait, but I'll be back soon as the theatre is dark and explain it all to you." Primrose paused, biting her lip. "Well, I guess there is something I'll tell you now. Stand up, Amelia, turn your back to me and close your eyes."

Was Primrose going to bring out her locket again? Should she be reminded that she had already shown it once? No, Amelia decided. She did not want to spoil a surprise, and would not say anything. She stood up without a word, turned, and squeezed her eyes shut.

"You . . . you can look now," said Primrose hesitantly.

Amelia turned back again. "Oh no!" she gasped.

"I'm sorry, Amelia. I didn't want to scare you. You're not going to faint or anything like that, are you?" said Primrose.

But no, it was not Primrose! Oh, the pink velveteen dress with the bouncing petticoats under it was there all right. But the golden curls, instead of being atop her head, had now become a wig held in her hand. The golden curls had been replaced by a thatch of tousled brown hair, and the head was now seen to be the head of the boy who had been sweeping in front of the theatre, the boy who had brought Amelia into the building, and then gone to "find" Primrose.

"I can't . . . I can't," began Amelia, but no more words would come.

"I would have told you aboard ship, but I didn't dare. And I never thought we'd see each other again," the boy said. "But my name is not really Primrose, except when I'm being the London canary. What they call me is Rosie."

Chapter XIII

A Proper Boy

"Amelia! Amelia!"

Hazily, Amelia heard her name being called, and stirred in her sleep.

"Amelia! Amelia!"

Again she heard her name being called, and she woke with a start. But where was she now? She was certainly not in her cabin bed on the ship. She was not in her barren cellar room. She was, instead, all curled up on the floor surrounded by mops and brooms. And who was that strange boy standing and staring at her? His bright blue eyes did look familiar.

"Primrose?" she murmured, her mind still fuzzy from a deep sleep.

"No, not Primrose, Amelia," the boy said. "It's Rosie now. You have to get used to that. Anyway, can't you see I'm not in my creeping Primrose costume?"

Amelia nodded sheepishly. Now fully awake, she could indeed see that Rosie was no longer in his pink velveteen dress and golden-curled wig, but was in a blue cotton shirt, blue corduroy knee pants, and black knee stockings. But did he not know how difficult it had been to discover that Primrose was a boy named Rosie?

"Creepers, Amelia, I'm sorry," he said. "I don't blame you for being mixed up about this. I'm also sorry it's so late, but I didn't dare come in sooner. I'm not surprised you fell asleep. But they've all gone now. I have to stay behind to clean up. Tooter used to do it himself, until I came along. Are you ready to hear my idea?"

Amelia scrambled up from the floor. "Oh yes!"

"Well," said Rosie, "it starts with you turning into a boy."

"A . . . a *boy*?" stammered Amelia.

"Yes, a *boy*, Amelia," said Rosie firmly. "Unless you wish to live in this broom closet, that's what you have to be, especially if you don't want Smeech and Turk to remember where they ever saw you before. If they did, then off you would no doubt go to Cousin Basil before we even had a chance to find out if that's where you want to go."

"But how do I become a boy?" asked Amelia.

"Easy as pie," said Rosie. "I get some scissors from the costume room and give you a nice hairdressing, which is to say, chop off your hair. Then I get a boy costume from the same location. You put it on, and there you are."

"But what happens after that, Prim . . . I mean, Rosie?" Amelia asked.

"What happens," replied Rosie, "is that I tell Tooter in the morning a boy came to the theatre while I was sweeping up. For food and a place to sleep inside, the boy said he would work here and stay all night to guard the theatre. I happen to know it's what Tooter wants because he wanted me to do that, on top of work-ing at being the London canary, mind you. I said I'd help cleaning up, but sleeping here would scare me so much I'd no doubt lose my voice. Course, no such thing, but I scared *Tooter* so much, that was the end of that." Rosie grinned. But his grin vanished as he looked anxiously at Amelia. "The problem is you *have* to stay here, Amelia. You can't stay in the boardinghouse round the corner where I stay with Smeech and Turk. They don't have ladies or girls there, and it's too risky besides. Would you be scared staying here?"

Scared? Of course Amelia would be scared! But had she not been alone at night in her cellar prison? Would this be any worse?

"Are . . . are there rats?" she asked, trying to keep her voice from trembling.

The grin returned at once to Rosie's face. "I don't think any rat would dare show its creeping whiskers around here, not with Choppers about."

"Choppers?" said Amelia. "Who is Choppers?"

"Real name is Mutton Chop," replied Rosie. "He's a big black cat with a white bib who thinks he owns this theatre. He's prowling around in the wings right now, I don't doubt."

"Well . . . " said Amelia uncertainly, then went on a little less uncertainly, "well, I guess I might not be quite so scared then."

"Whew!" said Rosie. "So now I'm off to get some scissors and your costume. Be right back!"

When Rosie returned, he had with him not only the scissors and a boy's outfit, but two old quilts as well, used for stage props, he explained. They were to serve as Amelia's bed in the broom closet. He also had with him a small brown paper sack.

"It's my supper," he said. "Lucky I didn't have time to eat it earlier, because I expect you haven't had anything for awhile."

"Not since last night," Amelia said.

"Creepers! I should have thought about it before," Rosie said. "Sorry, this isn't much though. Just some cheese and bread. But guess what, Amelia . . . an apple!"

"An apple!" Amelia could not keep from clapping her hands with delight. "Do you know all I've had for four days is just what you had in steerage, Rosie—porridge, bread, and grease. Oh, how I wished someone would bring *me* an apple."

"Well, now someone has!" Rosie grinned, made a deep Primrose-style curtsy, and handed Amelia the apple.

The meal ended, Amelia remained seated on her bucket, while

Rosie pushed up his sleeves with a great flourish, preparing to cut her hair. Yet he no sooner had his sleeves up than he quickly pulled them down again. It was too late. The shocked look on Amelia's face told him that she had already seen the ugly black bruise on his arm, the one that had been covered by the big puffed sleeves of his Primrose costume. His face reddened.

"I didn't mean for you to see that, Amelia. It . . . it's nothing much. It's just where Smeech walloped me."

This did not seem like "nothing much" to Amelia. "Walloped you!" she cried. "But why?"

"Do you remember on the ship when I told you that Smeech and Turk wouldn't want to feed me to the sharks as long as I stayed their little canary?" Rosie asked.

Amelia nodded. She also remembered thinking that Cousin Charlotte might have had the same in mind for her as well. But she had never been struck in her life, not even by Cousin Charlotte.

"Well," Rosie continued, "anytime Smeech or Turk hear a crack in my voice . . . or *think* they hear it, because it's all in their heads . . . they get so afraid their little canary's going to grow up and turn into a creeping crow, they like to remind the canary it better not think about doing that." Rosie paused, clearly fighting back tears. "It's not going to happen for awhile yet, but one day I'll grow up, and nobody can do anything about it . . . not Smeech, not Turk, not even me. Meantime, between now and then, I'll just have to be getting a lot of wallops."

"Can't you run away?" asked Amelia, horrified.

"I'm like you," Rosie replied simply. "Where would I run?"

This conversation cast a deep silence over the broom closet for a few moments.

"No more about that," Rosie said finally. "Nothing I can do about it, and I have to get back or they'll come looking for me. So, on with the haircut!"

Snip! Snip! Snip! Soon long strands of chestnut-brown hair had parted from Amelia's head and floated down to the floor. She could not help but feel sad, remembering how Papa had so loved her long hair, and how Polly had so proudly piled it atop her head. Now it lay all around her, ready for nothing but to be swept away. Yet even though the results of Rosie's handiwork could best be described as "shaggy," Amelia could not remain sad when she saw the pleased look on his face as he held up the small mirror brought from the costume room so she could see her new self.

"You do look a proper boy, Amelia," Rosie said proudly. And he said the same thing yet again when he stepped back into the broom closet after leaving Amelia to climb into her boy's costume of shirt and cotton britches. "Nobody would know you in a million years! Now all that's left is to give you a proper boy name."

Sam—that was the name they decided upon, and it was Rosie's idea. He had added an "S" to Amelia's name, and subtracted the last four letters, which ended up being Sam. "Makes it easier to remember if we have a connection," he said. "But we have to practice. I shall even call you that when we're by ourselves. One slip in front of Smeech and Turk, and . . . " He drew a telling finger across his throat.

This last matter settled, Rosie consulted his battered nickel pocket watch. "Wheeooo!" he whistled. "It's way past midnight, Am . . . oops!" This time he wiped imaginary perspiration from his forehead. "I mean, *Sam*. Creepers, I'd best not do that again! Anyway, I ought not to stay any longer. I can finish my cleaning in the morning. I'll be here before the sun is even up. I promise. Will you be all right?" he asked anxiously.

Amelia nodded.

"Sure?" said Rosie.

"Oh yes!" said Amelia, forcing a small smile.

"Well, good night then . . . *Sam*," Rosie said. And with another cheerful grin, he was gone.

Amelia was now alone in the Castle Theatre. Alone with only a dim lamp fluttering in the hallway outside the broom closet where she would be sleeping. Alone, knowing that just beyond where she slept was a cavernous stage, now dark and empty but echoing with the ghostly voices of the thousand actors who had walked across its boards. Amelia, alone and wishing she had told Rosie no, she was not going to be all right. Not for one tiny, terror-stricken moment would she be all right.

But how could she have done such a thing? She had descended upon him with no warning, and he was doing the very best he could. Further, he was helping her at terrible risk to himself. How could anyone seeing the bruise on his arm not know that? For what if Smeech and Turk were to discover that he was secretly hiding Amelia? No, spending the nights in the theatre was the only solution, and Rosie would not be told that she was not "all right."

Yet oh, it was not going to be easy. Behind the closed door of the darkened broom closet, Amelia pulled the quilt up around her shoulders and kept her eyes squeezed shut. But she could not fall asleep. Was the building trying to scare her with its old timbers creaking and groaning all around her? Or was that someone out there making those sounds? Wait! What was it? What was that scratching sound at her door?

Rat!

Please, let it not be a rat! Amelia pleaded silently. But the scratching continued. Then suddenly it stopped, and was followed by a loud, plaintive meow!

Amelia instantly scrambled up from the floor and opened the door. Standing there was an enormous black cat with a white bib, bent tail, and ears that had clearly seen battle action in an alley or two. But nothing had ever looked so wonderful to Amelia.

"Choppers!" she cried.

Choppers, for it was indeed he, walked in, not at all concerned that he had not yet been invited, and wrapped himself several times around Amelia's ankles. Then he strolled over to her quilt, sniffed about for the warmest spot, which was directly in the middle, lay down on it, and looked up at Amelia as if to say, "Well, what are you going to do about this?"

Did Amelia have a choice? Of course not! She kneeled down and rubbed the cat's battle-scarred ears, then lay gently down on the few remaining inches of quilt allowed to her. To the sound of the cat's loud purring, which seemed to drown out all the old theatre could produce in the way of scary sound effects, Amelia finally drifted off to sleep.

And that is how Rosie found them when he arrived in the morning.

Chapter XIV

Caught in the Very Act!

"So your name is Sam, eh?" said Alberforce Q. Tooter. His jowls, the color of a pale-pink ham, quivered as he took a large, oozing bite of a custard-filled doughnut, all the while staring at Amelia through small, squinting eyes.

"Y . . . y . . . yes." Amelia barely heard her voice replying faintly. Her legs were trembling so hard it was all she could do to stay upright and not end up a crumpled heap on the floor.

She was facing a lineup of gentlemen composed not only of Mr. Alberforce Q. Tooter, but Mr. Thessalonius Smeech and Mr. Alphonso Turk as well. It was, of course, the first she had ever seen of Mr. Tooter. But oh, how different Mr. Smeech and Mr. Turk appeared from the time she had first seen them.

No longer the jolly, twinkling teller of jokes with a big blossom in his buttonhole, Mr. Smeech looked crabbed and ill-humored, his formerly ruddy face sagging and pallid as an unbaked pastry. And could this man with the sullen, stubbled face, whose bored eyelids drooped over eyes as sharp as those of any fox, be the dashing, heartthrobbing Mr. Turk, who had brought tears to Amelia's eyes with his rendering of "The Little Orphans"? Now it seemed possible to believe everything Primrose—now Rosie—had said about them.

"What's your last name, Sam?" asked Mr. Smeech, his eyes popping as he thrust his head forward to fix Amelia with a suspicious stare.

"It . . . it . . . " began Amelia, and then came to a dead stop. What *was* her last name to be? Why had she and Rosie not even thought about that?

"It's . . . it's *Smith!*" Rosie piped up from the sidelines. "Sam Smith. That's what he told me."

"Sam Smith?" Mr. Turk gave a twisted grin. "That's original enough. That really your name, Sam?"

"Oh y . . . yes, s . . . sir," said Amelia.

"I detect a bit of an English accent there," said Mr. Smeech. "Where did that come from?"

"I . . . I . . . " Amelia began, stopping again as her heart lodged itself firmly in her throat. How many more questions were there to be that she was not prepared for?

"Uh," said Rosie, jumping in again. "I thought I'd said. His ma who died was English."

"Look here, Rosie," said Mr. Tooter, "can't this boy speak for himself?"

"Sorry," said Rosie, becoming the very picture of sheepish discomfort.

"Makes me wonder how much good he'll be if he lets you speak for him," growled Mr. Tooter. "Maybe you'd better stay with the cleaning job yourself, Rosie."

In less time than it took for an eye to wink, Rosie broke out in a violent fit of coughing. Dancing about, he clutched his throat, choking and gurgling as if each breath was his last. He even managed to turn an impressive red into the bargain. "All right, Tooter, you can see what all this dusting is doing to my tonsils," he croaked. "But if you wish to shoot an arrow right through the throat of your canary, that's up to you."

Mr. Tooter turned and shrugged at Mr. Smeech, who shrugged back. So splendid was Rosie's performance that who would dare challenge it?

"Oh, never mind then," snapped Mr. Tooter testily. "But you're certain Sam knows all he's to get is food, which you'll be bringing him, and this roof over his head, for which he's to do the cleaning up and stay with the theatre all night?"

"It's what he says," replied Rosie.

"That right, Sam?" said Mr. Tooter.

Amelia nodded. "Y . . . yes, sir."

Mr. Tooter studied the last bite of his custard doughnut, threw it into his mouth, and then carefully licked each finger of the operative hand, all before replying. "Then you can get started today," he grunted. "Rosie will show you what's to be done."

"One moment, Tooter," Mr. Smeech broke in. "I'd like to ask Sam here a question." He gave Mr. Tooter and Mr. Turk each a knowing sideways look. Then he turned back to Amelia with narrowed eyes. "You ever done any singing, Sam?"

"Oh yes, sir! When I was in . . . when I was in . . . " Amelia's voice faded into frozen silence.

"When you were in what?" said Mr. Smeech, his face alight with greedy pleasure. After all, here might be a second canary in the making. "Go on! Go on!"

Go on? Go on with *what*? How could Amelia go on when what she had been about to announce was that her singing had taken place in Mrs. Draper's music class! Why was Rosie not coming to her rescue again? It was clear from the benign, satisfied look on his face, however, that he had no idea Amelia even needed rescuing.

After a few moments of unrelieved terror, Amelia was miraculously able to rescue herself. "I . . . I . . . I used to sing when I was scrubbing floors!" she blurted. Well, had Annie the housemaid not done just that when down on her hands and knees in their London kitchen?

"That's all? Just sung when you were doing the kitchen floors?" Mr. Smeech's pasty face was now scarlet with anger at having been made to look foolish.

"Y . . . yes, s . . . sir," said Amelia.

"Why don't you let him try a song, Smeech?" Rosie asked cheerily.

"Why not, Smeech?" said Mr. Tooter. "Sing us something, Sam."

"What . . . what shall I sing?" asked Amelia.

"How about one of Rosie's favorites, 'Believe Me If All Those Endearing Young Charms'?" volunteered Mr. Turk with a mocking grin.

"I . . . I don't know that," stammered Amelia.

"What a surprise!" said Mr. Turk.

"Then sing what you do know," snapped Mr. Smeech.

By now Amelia felt as if she were trying to hold herself up on two legs made of rapidly melting jelly. But she took a breath and began to sing, in a voice so tiny and quavering it could barely be heard, the only song she could remember. Alas, it was one from her earliest singing days at Mrs. Draper's Academy.

> "Little Bo-Peep has lost her sheep,
> And doesn't know where to find them.
> Leave them alone, and they'll come home,
> Dragging their tails behind them.
>
> Little Bo-Peep fell fast asleep,
> And dreamt she heard them bleating.
> But when she awoke, she found it a joke,
> For they were still a-fleeting."

When the performance had ended, it was greeted with a deadly silence.

"Well, so much for that grand idea," said Mr. Turk.

"I hope he sweeps better than he sings," said Mr. Tooter.

"Rosie, you take him in hand," snarled Mr. Smeech. "Maybe you can do something about it."

"Your wish is my command, Smeech," said Rosie, with a curtsy, and triumphant grin at Amelia.

Swish! Swish! Swish! The brooms swept across the stage, their whispering sounds floating up and disappearing into the rafters and the vast, eerie darkness of the theatre auditorium. Only a pair of tiny lamps flickered weakly on the back wall of the stage, barely enough to light up the two sweepers and a large black cat slinking soft-pawed and silent behind the flats. Mr. Tooter's pinch-penny ways saw to it that, but for the two aforementioned lamps, the theatre should remain as dark as possible when not officially in use. It was in truth Mr. Tooter and company who were under discussion by the sweepers at that very moment. And oh, how happy one of them, Amelia, was that Rosie, the other, under pretext of supervising her work—as well as instructing her in the art of singing—could be with her in that theatre as dark and filled with echoes as the deepest cave.

"I told you all people in the theatre aren't like Smeech and Turk and Tooter," Rosie said. "My pa wasn't, just as I told you. And most people in the theatre would give you their last penny, if you needed it."

"I know," replied Amelia, who in the few days she had been employed by Mr. Tooter and company had met some extraordinarily nice warmhearted people. They seemed to delight in patting her on the head and calling her "a good boy" whenever she helped them out in even the smallest ways. Because of this, and because she was with Rosie so much of the time, not to mention the company of Choppers at night, Amelia was not nearly so frightened as she had been. Still, there was something that continued to worry her.

"Rosie, I've been thinking," she said. "Don't you think I ought to try to find out about Cousin Charlotte and Cousin Basil? I mean, what if there's a proper explanation for all that happened, and they're trying to find me."

Rosie stopped sweeping and leaned on his broom. "I've been thinking about it too, Sam, and I have a plan. Smeech has a little green book where he keeps notes on just about everything. I expect if he did get hold of the address for where your Cousin Basil lives, that's where it would be. I'm going to get it and then go exploring. I find pennies when I sweep up, and I have them hidden away. They'll do for tram rides, which I expect will be needed. When I get there, I'll try to find out if anyone is looking for a little girl who's ended up missing."

"What if no one is?" asked Amelia, a catch in her voice.

"Then it's no different from where it all was before, Sam," Rosie said gently. "Anyway, if it turns up you're staying right here, then we'd better work hard on your singing lessons. You ought not to have to end up sweeping the rest of your days. And today's the day, I've decided, you're going to try singing on stage."

"Oh no!" Amelia cried. "I can't!"

"Oh yes, you can," said Rosie. "You can't keep on singing in the broom closet. Now, you stay up here, and I'll go sit in the front row."

As Rosie jumped down from the stage and settled himself in a front row seat, Amelia laid down her broom and, feet dragging, approached the front of the stage.

"Let's hear 'Believe Me,'" Rosie called up to her.

"You know I haven't learned all the words yet," complained Amelia.

"Then sing as far as you know," Rosie returned cheerfully. "Come on now!"

Clasping her hands in front of herself, and taking three deep breaths for courage, Amelia began to sing. Her voice was so tiny and trembling, it seemed it must come from a bird even smaller than a canary. But she never did miss a note, and when she had finished the first verse, which was all she knew, Rosie leaped up and began clapping and whistling.

"Good girl! You'll soon show them, Amelia!" he shouted. "Ooops! I mean, Sam!" he quickly corrected himself. But not quickly enough.

Suddenly, the brilliant white lights of all the gas lamps flared up across the front of the stage. Blinded by the glare, Amelia could no longer even see Rosie in the darkness beyond them, nor anyone else. But she could hear the voice of Mr. Smeech.

"Caught in the very act! I thought there was something fishy about this whole thing. Sam, indeed! How did you come up with this one, Rosie?" he shouted furiously. "What is it you think you're getting away with?"

The next thing Amelia knew, Mr. Smeech had snapped his big hand like a steel handcuff around Rosie's arm, and was dragging him up onto the stage. Behind them sauntered Mr. Turk. Mr. Smeech had an arm raised as if ready to send Rosie hurtling across the stage, but Mr. Turk quickly tapped Mr. Smeech on the shoulder.

"Don't go killing the canary, Smeech," he muttered. "Not yet, anyway."

Mr. Smeech let his arm drop, but still looked ready to burst with rage. "So let's have an explanation, and it had better be a good one. What's your little friend doing here, Rosie? And what exactly was your part in this?"

Rosie did not answer. He just stared back at Mr. Smeech with his jaw stubbornly shut.

"Am I going to have to beat it out of you?" Mr. Smeech's hand tightened around Rosie's arm.

Rosie might be defiant, but Amelia could see the fear in his eyes. She herself was paralyzed with fright, but she could not stand there and let Rosie take the blame for something she had done. She *would* not!

"It . . . it . . . it was not Rosie's fault!" she cried out. "I came here, and he never even knew I was coming."

"Ah, the little bird *does* have a voice," said Mr. Turk.

"Is what she says true?" Mr. Smeech gave Rosie's arm a shake.

Rosie stared at the toes of his shoes, continuing his stubborn silence. Another shake of his arm, however, produced a reluctant nod.

"What brought you here, Miss Fairwick?" asked Mr. Smeech. "It is Amelia Fairwick, is it not?"

"I . . . I ran away." Amelia blurted.

"Ran away?" inquired Mr. Smeech. "You mean you ran away from the lady you were with on the ship?"

Amelia shook her head.

"Well, then *who*?" Mr. Smeech glared at her threateningly.

"I . . . I . . . I . . . " began Amelia. And then it all became too much for her at last. To her horror and dismay, she burst into tears.

Holding his silence now became too much for Rosie. "Don't you go bullying her, Smeech!" he burst out. "She was kidnapped, that's what she was! When her cousin went off someplace, somebody came up to her friendly as you please and invited her to where they lived. Then they went and locked her up. But she escaped and came here because she doesn't know where her cousin lives. And if you want to know what I think, I think those people were off to get ransom!"

"Ransom?" said Mr. Smeech. His eyebrows slithered up his forehead as he exchanged significant glances with Mr. Turk. It was instantly clear now that Rosie had gone too far in his brave speech.

"Ransom, eh?" repeated Mr. Smeech with narrowed, calculating eyes. "But of course now if old Mother Hubbard, namely the cousin, goes there, she will find the cupboard bare, so to speak. Isn't that right, Turk?"

"Which means," replied Mr. Turk, rubbing his chin thoughtfully, "we are now talking reward instead of ransom."

"Precisely," said Mr. Smeech. "Of course, there might be one little problem. What if the cousin thinks *we* are the kidnappers?"

"Oh, I don't believe that will be any problem at all," replied Mr. Turk smoothly. Turning on his most charming stage-idol smile, he said to Amelia, "Now, Miss Fairwick here knows full well we are not the kidnappers, and that we never were. She knows that we are, to put it simply, her rescuers. I think she would find it most difficult to lie about such a matter. Isn't that so, Miss Fairwick?"

Wide eyes locked on Mr. Turk, Amelia nodded not once, but twice, like a little puppet on a string.

Mr. Turk repeated his smile. "Then no more need be said about it."

This matter settled, Mr. Smeech jerked his head at Mr. Turk, and the two stepped off a few feet away from Amelia and Rosie.

"Before we take her there, shouldn't we find out what kind of reward's being offered?" Mr. Smeech asked in what could only be called a stage whisper. For unless he thought Rosie and Amelia were deaf, every word he uttered could be clearly heard.

"What for?" asked Mr. Turk.

"Because," replied Mr. Smeech, "if we don't know what it is, they might just give us a portion, and we'd never be the wiser."

"You have a point," said Mr. Turk. "And I suppose the way to find out about it would be to see what's posted at the police station. Shall I go, or shall you?"

"You go," said Mr. Smeech. "I'll stay here and see that there's no more escaping being done."

"What about Tooter?" asked Mr. Turk.

"What about him?" replied Mr. Smeech.

"Should we tell him about this?" said Mr. Turk.

"He's got to know the second bird has flown the coop," Mr. Smeech said. "But why tell him about the reward? Why should he get something he had nothing to do with getting?"

Mr. Turk gave his familiar twisted grin. "Why indeed, Smeech?" he said.

"Creeping creepers! How could I have been so stupid, giving them that idea about ransom?" Rosie quietly exploded as they entered the costume room where they had been sent by Mr. Smeech to find "something respectable" for Amelia to wear when she was delivered into the hands of her cousin.

"You wouldn't have said anything at all if I hadn't cried," said Amelia. "*That's* what was stupid."

"See here," Rosie said, "you were entitled, Mr. Smeech scaring you like that. I probably would have been crying as well except that I'm used to them by now. But what's stupider than all of it put together was me forgetting to call you Sam. And to think how scared I was it was *you* might be going to make the mistake." Rosie shook his head. "Think of it, all along there were the two of them lurking in the wings!"

"It doesn't matter, Rosie," Amelia said at once. "Mr. Smeech was suspicious all along, he said, and they probably would have found out anyway."

"Maybe," said Rosie. "But not right away. Then I would have had time to learn what I could about your cousins. I still think there's something fishy about all of it. And what if I'm right? What will you do then?"

"I don't know. But . . . but I'm certain everything will end all right," Amelia said. She wanted to hide from Rosie how truly frightened she was, for what could he do to help her now? But it was impossible to keep her voice from trembling.

"Creepers!" Rosie said. "What am I doing scaring you half to death? I'm sorry, truly I am. I think everything will end all right, too. But I'm coming around to make certain it does. I don't know how I'll manage it, but I will somehow. And that's a creeping promise, Sam!"

Chapter XV

Doomed!

Clop! Clop! Clop!

Once again Amelia sat on the chilling black leather seat of a cab, feet crossed and hands folded, listening to the leaden drumming of horses' hooves that were carrying her to—what? What and whom would she find when they arrived at their destination? And what might someone think of her looking as she did, with her shorn head, and wearing the same ugly dress and coat in which she had first arrived at the Castle Theatre? For in the end, the costume room could offer nothing that fit her. It had, however, provided a broad-brimmed cherry-red velveteen hat, laden with flowers and feathers, and totally unsuitable for a child her age. It was now pulled down over her ears in an attempt to cover as much of her head as possible.

In curious contrast to Amelia, wearing this outlandish hat, sat two remarkably somber gentlemen, so somber one would have found it almost impossible to recognize them as Mr. Thessalonius Smeech and Mr. Alphonso Turk. Both were in sober black suits and hats, ransacked without a doubt from the selfsame costume room of the Castle Theatre. Mr. Turk might well have passed for a staid businessman. Mr. Smeech, on the other hand, had found himself a clerical collar and had transformed himself into the Reverend Smeech. In any event, that was how Amelia was told she should address him should the matter come up.

After some distance traveled in silence, Mr. Turk finally spoke. "I still say, Smeech, we might have sent a letter first. What does this look like, us just showing up on the doorstep? But you were in such an almighty hurry."

"And I still say there was no sense in waiting around for letters," snapped Mr. Smeech. "Besides, as I pointed out, the longer we wait, the better chance for Tooter to find out what's going on and demand his share."

"Well, at the moment it's a share of nothing," said Mr. Turk. "We don't even know if there *is* a reward. It was your idea, after all, that we should find out about it before merely appearing there like a pair of simpletons."

"You can't say we didn't try," returned Mr. Smeech. "And it was you who found out that there was not so much as a peep about it at the police station, nor even a sign posted."

"It's odd indeed," said Mr. Turk. "Not one person there knew a thing about it."

"Which is exactly the reason for this costume," said Mr. Smeech triumphantly. "Brilliant idea, if I do say so myself. It should certainly loosen the purse strings, or my name isn't Reverend Smeech."

"Which of course it isn't," retorted Mr. Turk dryly.

This remark, needless to say, sent the Reverend Smeech into a sulky silence for some time.

The conversation, every word of it heard by Amelia, caused the skin on her neck to creep. She had never thought about notices in a police station. Now she knew about them, and was hearing for the first time that there was "not so much as a peep" there about her. What more positive proof could there be that her being deserted at the docks was intended, and that she was not wanted by either cousin? Yet here she was being drawn helplessly nearer and nearer to them. Clop! Clop! Clop! How much more deadly had the sound of the horses' hooves become!

Snowflakes had begun to fall as the horses' hooves slowed and the cab turned into a wide, circular driveway. Through the window, Amelia found herself looking up past the flakes at an enormous house of grey stone, with a turret rising up one side, making the house look every bit like a miniature castle. Perhaps in the summer when framed by the leaves of oak and willow trees, and roses along the driveway, or even bright holiday decorations, the house might not look so forbidding. As it was, it seemed only a pile of cold grey stone with bleak, darkened windows.

But still, it was a large, imposing house, and when his eyes fell upon it, Mr. Turk gave a long, low whistle. "Wheeooo!"

"Money! Money! Money!" said Mr. Smeech in a reverent voice.

"You know, Smeech," said Mr. Turk, "we should have taken her out and bought her some proper clothes. What do you suppose they'll think of these rags?"

"Never mind," said Mr. Smeech. "You will explain that once you discovered who the child was, you spoke to your good friend . . . myself . . . and I said she must be returned as quickly as possible, never mind shopping for clothes. Anyway, here we are!"

The cab had drawn up and stopped before the broad stone steps leading up to the house. As soon as the driver opened the door, Mr. Smeech and Mr. Turk came close to falling rather than stepping out as they shoved through the door. In their greedy hurry they almost forgot Amelia, who was left to scramble down behind them in the best way she could.

Ordering the cab driver to wait, the two gave Amelia an impatient push, and raced up the steps. There Mr. Smeech gave a politely delicate tap-tap on the surprisingly tarnished brass knocker that hung on the massive oak door. When no one appeared, he tap-tapped again, a little louder and a little less delicately polite. A few moments passed, and then the door was cautiously opened. It revealed a man with a sharp, sallow face, who studied them with narrowed, appraising eyes.

"Yes?" he said coldly. "May I inquire what it is you wish?"

Mr. Smeech drew himself up to his pompous best. "I would like to present myself. I am the Reverend Thessalonius Smeech, and this is my friend Mr. Alphonso Turk. We are here to see Mr. Basil Desmond on a matter which we believe to be of extreme importance to him, namely the return of his young cousin, Amelia Fairwick, whom you see here before you."

At the conclusion of these remarks, the man looked sharply at Amelia, then quickly opened the door wider and stepped back. "Please enter," he said. "I shall summons Mr. Desmond at once."

Mr. Smeech and Mr. Turk, together with Amelia, then stepped through the doorway and into a vast hall, chilly and dank as a stone vault. "Grand" might have been the word used to describe the room once. Now the wan light from three small gas lamps flickered from the walls over dusty cobwebs that hung in dense drapes from the two unlit crystal chandeliers overhead. Curious stains on the bare walls, upon closer look, were seen to be in the shape of picture frames no longer there. And whereas marks on the faded, threadbare Persian carpet revealed the former presence of other chairs and tables, only two chairs, decorated with tarnished gold braid, remained to stand like forlorn sentries beside the front door.

Still, the room was impressive with its great oak beams crossing a fourteen-foot-high ceiling, splendid carved wood moldings, and magnificent stairway curving up the wall. And though the general air of desolation, neglect, and gloom hanging over the room like a pall plunged Mr. Smeech and Mr. Turk into sudden silence, the looks of greedy expectation never left their faces. Their sharp eyes eagerly watched the man tread silently away through French doors leading to an adjoining parlor, and then disappear through another door at the far end.

It was but a few minutes before he reappeared, following behind another man, who strode across the parlor and entered the hall where Mr. Smeech, Mr. Turk, and Amelia stood waiting. But Amelia's eyes had no sooner fallen on the man than her blood turned to ice.

Glacial blue eyes—sharp nose, chin, and cheekbones—deadly pale skin. If the figure standing before them were wearing a black veiled hat covering all his straight dark hair, and a severe black dress instead of his stern black suit, Cousin Basil—for indeed it was he—might very well pass for Cousin Charlotte!

"Well, is this the girl?" he asked abruptly, in a voice so like that of Cousin Charlotte's Amelia could not have told the difference for her life. His eyes had barely flicked past her before he addressed Mr. Smeech and Mr. Turk.

"Oh, oh, oh yes, it is indeed, Mr. Desmond!" replied Mr. Smeech, an oily smile creasing his face.

"And we do apologize for her garments," Mr. Turk broke in quickly. "But we felt that, once we learned of her identity, we should deliver her to you as quickly as possible, and not take the time to have her suitably outfitted. These are, however, the garments she arrived in, although the hat came from our costume department. I, of course, am connected to the theatre, and my friend here, as you can see, is a man of the cloth." Mr. Turk paused at this point to allow Mr. Smeech to fold his hands and look soulfully heavenward.

"And do allow me to present ourselves," continued Mr. Turk. "I am Mr. Alphonso Turk and this is the Reverend Thessalonius Smeech."

"Yes, yes, yes," said Cousin Basil, nodding curtly to each of the men. "What I should like to know, however, is how she came to be with you?"

Mr. Turk cleared his throat importantly. "A simple enough explanation, Mr. Desmond. Believing herself to have been abandoned at the docks upon her arrival, she accepted the invitation of someone purporting to be of help, but who, alas, took her to their residence and imprisoned her. She managed to escape and, not knowing your whereabouts it appears, was able to make her way to the only person and place she knew of, who was Primrose at the Castle Theatre, Primrose being her friend from the ship as well as a member of our little theatrical troupe from London. Upon hearing her story, it seemed instantly clear to us that what those despicable villains were after was ransom from yourself." Mr. Turk sketched a slight bow after concluding this speech, almost as if he expected applause from a theatre audience.

He might as well have been delivering the better part of it to a stone monument, however, for there was no expression on Cousin Basil's face whatsoever, except perhaps at the very end when his eyes narrowed a fraction.

"Ransom, eh?" he said after a barely measurable pause. "Well, you were quite correct in that. Of course, the girl should have remained where she was taken, for I was led there by her captors only to find her gone. But I should like to know how you knew where to bring her when she, as you said, did not know my whereabouts?"

"Oh, I discovered that when aboard the *Sylvania*," said Mr. Turk, quickly adding, "quite inadvertently of course."

"And for which we may be ever thankful," said Mr. Smeech, sending another look heavenward.

"Yes, I suppose we may," said Cousin Basil impatiently. "At any rate, thank you, gentlemen, for delivering the girl to me. Now, if you will excuse me, Mr. Quinge will show you out."

Mr. Smeech and Mr. Turk exchanged panic-stricken glances. "Excuse me please, Mr. Desmond," said Mr. Turk, "but you failed to tell us. Was any ransom in fact paid to the dastardly kidnappers?"

"None at all," replied Cousin Basil coolly. "I simply outwitted them."

"But . . . but . . . but have you offered no reward for her return?" blurted Mr. Turk, his face growing paler by the moment.

"None," said Cousin Basil. "I was fully confident that I could secure her return without resorting to such measures. It appears that I was right, does it not?"

"But . . . but . . . but," sputtered Mr. Smeech, nearly choking on his clerical collar, "perhaps you might like to consider a contribution to . . . to the church, by way of . . . of gratitude for her safe return. And . . . and with so little effort on your part, I might add."

"A contribution to the church?" Cousin Basil's right eyebrow lifted slightly. "I believe that might be arranged. Quinge, as you see these gentlemen out, you will please get from the Reverend Smeech the name of his church. Next Sunday, I shall see that something worthy of his efforts finds its way to the collection plate. Now, I bid you good-day, gentlemen."

The meeting had ended so swiftly and abruptly that Mr. Smeech and Mr. Turk could do nothing but meekly allow Mr. Quinge to usher them to the door. Before they reached it, however, the startled looks on their faces had rapidly turned to a seething mixture of disappointment, indignation—and rage.

"Quinge," Cousin Basil said no sooner than the door had closed behind the two men, "you may put her in the green room, and warn her that she is not to go wandering. Someone will see her shortly with further instructions. When you return, please see me in my study." With that he turned on his heels to leave the hall. Was he going to do so without so much as a word to Amelia?

"C . . . C . . . Cousin Basil!" she cried out, her heart pounding.

He hesitated and stopped, but did not turn around. "Yes?"

Amelia had no idea what she intended to say, so said the first thing that came into her mind. "What . . . whatever happened to Cousin Charlotte?"

Cousin Basil shrugged. "I have not the remotest idea," he said, his voice completely expressionless. "I suggest you forget about her. Now Mr. Quinge will show you to your room." Then, never once having turned back to look at Amelia, he continued on his way across the parlor.

Numbly, Amelia followed the silent Mr. Quinge up the curving staircase and down a long hall to a small room at the very farthest end. The room had earned its name of "green room" by virtue of having dull green walls and a green rag rug on the floor. It contained only the plainest wood chair, dresser, small bed table, and iron cot imaginable. Tucked away as it was at the back of the house, the room had no doubt been a maid's room. But that hardly mattered to Amelia.

All that mattered was that Cousin Basil had not spoken her name once, or looked at her directly after his eyes had flicked past her when he first entered the hall. And *this* was the person who was to be her guardian. *This* was the person who was to have sole charge of her life. *This* was the person with whom she must live. And it seemed that right from the beginning, despite all the twists and turns in her journey, she had been doomed to end up right where she was. Doomed to end up in the hands of Cousin Basil.

Cousin Basil, who was as cold and cruelly indifferent to her as had been Cousin Charlotte. Cousin Basil, who had said he had "not the remotest idea" where Cousin Charlotte was, and told Amelia to forget about her. And Amelia knew why. For it was certain that the Cousin Charlotte who had brought her from London, who had deserted her on the docks, and who looked enough like Cousin Basil to be his twin, was in very fact—Cousin Basil himself!

Chapter XVI

A Welcome Night Visitor

Amelia started when a short while later she heard a knock at her door. Could this be once again the tight-lipped, silent Mr. Quinge, whom she already held in dread? But when she opened the door, all she found standing in the hall was a young girl, perhaps only a few years older than Amelia herself.

"It's Sarah the housemaid, come to give instructions to the young miss. Washroom's next door," the girl said in a timid little voice. She was in truth failing miserably at an attempt to sound as if she were used to giving instructions every day of her life. Her pale, faded blue eyes gave promise of being fixed permanently into an anxious, wide-eyed stare. Even the maid's cap set primly and properly over her lank yellow hair did nothing to dispel the appearance of her being overawed at finding herself in her situation.

"And . . . and excuse me, miss," she went on, "but I'm to say you're not to go snooping into any room that has doors closed. And . . . and excuse me again, miss, but I'm asked particularly to warn you're not to go exploring down the hall at the other end, though why you would want to is not for me to say." Sarah's eyes widened even further at having allowed such a bold observation to pop out of her mouth. Then she rushed on. "And . . . and the last thing is your supper's served at seven in the dining room. You'll hear the big clock downstairs go bonging, so you can't miss it."

She started to leave, then stopped, turned, and blurted, "Oh, excuse me another time, miss, but that is such a pretty hat you have on. I do love it!" Then she scurried off before Amelia had time to reward her with a grateful smile.

How Amelia wished Sarah could have stayed just a little longer. At the very least, she could have been assured that Amelia had no intention of going exploring in that grim stone house. She was far more frightened of it than Sarah had ever thought of being!

Bong! Bong! Bong! Bong! Bong! Bong! Bong! Somewhere far off in the house the clock tolled the hour. Amelia knew that she must now make her way to the dining room. Dreading the journey, she entered the hushed hall lit only by three palely fluttering gaslights, that stretched out so far it was finally swallowed up by deep shadows. No, nobody needed to warn Amelia against exploring!

The whole house, in truth, was dark and silent. Where was everyone? Was Mr. Quinge lurking in the shadows making certain she did as she had been told? And what of Cousin Basil? What if she came upon him as he prowled the halls? Cousin Basil! How was it going to feel sitting at the dining table with him? Would he finally have to look at Amelia? To speak to her? But when she reached the cavernous dining room, directly off the vast hall, she found a long dining table with six chairs around it—and only one place set! Had Sarah made a mistake? Was this place set for Cousin Basil alone? As Amelia stood there motionless, not knowing what she was expected to do, the door at the far end of the room burst open, and Sarah flew in.

"Go ahead and sit down, miss," she said, running up to Amelia breathlessly. "Mr. Quinge is tending to the master, so seems I'm to wait on you."

Now Amelia had the answer to her questions. The place was set for her, and she was to eat alone. Cousin Basil would have his meal at a later hour because he could not even bear to sit with her at the same table! As she slowly trailed over to her place, it seemed her spirits could not sink much lower.

But as she sat picking at her supper, which, while far better than the meals Rosie had been bringing her in paper sacks, did nothing to tempt her appetite, she heard the sound of low voices coming from the hall. Looking up, she saw Cousin Basil in black overcoat and hat opening the front door. He carried a traveling bag in one hand, and behind him came Mr. Quinge carrying another. Both men left the house. A few minutes later, Mr. Quinge returned empty-handed. From the outside came the sound of a carriage being drawn away. Cousin Basil, it appeared, had gone. Gone where, and why, and for how long? Even though Amelia was in terror of Cousin Basil, he was after all, her cousin and her guardian, and this was more than she could bear.

She waited until she no longer heard Mr. Quinge's footsteps in the hall. Then, with tears already streaming down her cheeks, she pushed herself away from the table and flew up the stairs to her room, gulping down sobs. But once again, just as when she had been alone in her cabin and in her cellar room, who was there to know or care? In that vast, grim house that was to be her new home, there was no one. No one!

Bong! Bong! Bong! The clock began to toll again. Curled up in her cot, eyes wide open, Amelia counted. Eleven! Already it was eleven o'clock at night, and she could not fall asleep. How could she with all that had happened spinning round in her head? What was to become of her? If Cousin Basil refused to have anything to do with her, what was she to do? How was she to spend her days?

Tap! Tap! Tap!

Amelia stiffened. Someone was at her door.

Tap! Tap! Tap! came again.

Amelia tried to steady her voice. "Who . . . who is it?"

"It's me, Sarah, miss," came the whispered reply.

Quickly, Amelia turned up her lamp and then climbed from her cot. Scrambling into her dress, she opened the door to find Sarah with a bowl in one hand, and something that appeared to be an article of clothing tucked under her arm. At her feet sat a small oil lantern, set down so she could tap on the door.

"I hope I didn't wake you, miss," she said in a hushed voice, "but I did have to wait until the light in Mr. Quinge's room was out before I could come. And I did tap ever so softly in case you were asleep. I thought you might not be, though, because . . . because . . . " she stumbled, "because, excuse me, miss, but I saw your tears as you went running from the dining room. And you left most all your supper, too. Anyway, thinking you might be sorry you'd left it, I brought it to you. I'm ever so sorry it's all slopped together in a bowl, miss. I had to do it quick-like. I didn't dare make a nice tray lest Mr. Quinge catch me at it. Mrs. McGregor . . . she's the cook . . . wouldn't mind a bit, but I expected Mr. Quinge would."

"Oh Sarah!" breathed Amelia. "It doesn't matter at all how it's served. I'm grateful to you. I truly am!"

"But, miss, I didn't mean to make you cry again!" Sarah said, stricken, for she had seen tears spring into Amelia's eyes.

"I'm not crying," Amelia said wholeheartedly. "I really am not, Sarah. It's only that I wasn't expecting such kindness."

Sarah's face flushed with pleasure. "Well, I'm ever so glad to do it. And . . . and excuse me, miss, but it appeared to me that you didn't have any traveling bag, and . . . and so might not have a sweater. I did have to ask Mr. Quinge if I could loan you one, thinking how he might know my sweater and would ask about it. But he just said it was nothing to him, and do it if I wanted to."

"Thank you ever so much, Sarah," Amelia said. "I will most

truly appreciate the sweater, as it is so very cold in this house."

"Small wonder with the radiators turned down past what all!" sniffed Sarah.

"But what will you wear then if I have your sweater?" asked Amelia.

"Oh, I have a second one," said Sarah proudly. "But I do have to go now. And . . . and, miss, if you'll excuse me for saying so, whatever caused your other tears will come round right. I know it will."

"I do hope so," said Amelia. "But . . . but I should like to ask you something. Do . . . do you know where my Cousin Basil has gone, or . . . or when he might return?"

"I don't know, miss, truly I don't!" Sarah's eyes, which had been sparkling ever since she arrived, were suddenly fear-stricken again. "And oh, excuse me, miss, but you must not ask me questions about goings-on here. And . . . and even if Mr. Quinge says I can do what I want with my sweater, I'm certain he wouldn't want us having conversations. So we mustn't be seen talking together. And what with Ma alone to take care of three little ones at home, I'm fortunate to have my situation here, not being able to do much else. I mustn't lose it. I must not!"

"I wouldn't want you to for anything," declared Amelia. "And I won't ask more questions. I promise I won't. But I would so love to have you come again for a visit whenever it's safe."

"I'll do that, miss, never you fear," said Sarah stoutly. "Only now I have to go. Breakfast is at eight and dinner at noon, in case I forgot to tell you. Good night, miss." With that she was gone.

Nothing had changed much. Amelia was still to live in that grey, gloomy house with a guardian who wanted nothing to do with her. But suddenly there was one great difference. For just as she had had the promise of Primrose on the ship, and Primrose who became Rosie at the Castle Theatre, Amelia now had Sarah. And it was the picture of Sarah's cheerful face that spun in her head as, at long last, she drifted off to sleep.

And how happy she was to have Sarah's warm sweater to put on when she arose the next morning! She already wore it as she leaned on the sill, looking out the window at the cold wintry sun. It had been rapidly darkening when she had arrived with Mr. Smeech and Mr. Turk the evening before, but she had seen enough to tell her the house must be surrounded by a large walled garden, as indeed it was. The trees and bushes, although lightly dusted with snowflakes, were bare of leaves. How lovely the garden would be in the spring!

But as Amelia looked out the window, she was surprised to see two figures rounding the corner from the back of the house and approaching down the brick path. Who could be out so early on this frigid morning? They appeared to be huddled in deep conversation. As they drew nearer, Amelia could see that one of the figures was Mr. Quinge. And the other—no, no, it could not be mistaken—the other was Mrs. Dobbins!

Chapter XVII

A Fearful Warning

Amelia warily opened the door of her room a few inches and peeked out. She had yet to get used to entering that dark, hushed hallway. Once, Mr. Quinge had terrified her by coming softly through one of the closed doors. Now, no matter where she crept in the house, she was always in fear of having him materialize before her. This was now her third morning in the house, yet she still could not open her door without feeling her skin prickle.

Slowly, carefully, she opened the door further, and then jumped back, her heart pounding. For the closed door opposite hers had begun to open. It opened further, and a hand came out and set down a bucket filled with rags. Oh, it must be Sarah coming out from cleaning the room! Amelia gave a sigh of relief as the door opened still further. Someone stood there with a mop, a broom, and dustpan, but it was not Sarah. It was Rosie!

"It's me!" he said cheerily. "I was wondering when I was going to run into you, Sam. I knew you were around someplace. I just didn't know where."

"Oh, Rosie!" breathed Amelia, almost too overcome with joy to speak. And then she gave a cry of horror. "Rosie, what's happened to you?" For she had now noticed the ugly black and purple bruise on his cheek and his red, swollen eye.

Rosie tried quickly to cover the bruise with his hand, but then just as quickly let it fall back to his side. "Can't very well hide this one, can I? But it happened the same way as before. Only difference is this time I had a place to run away to. Seems as if you ran away to me once. Now I've run away to you."

"I'm so glad you did, Rosie!" Amelia said. "I'm so glad!"

"Well," said Rosie, with a rueful grin. "I guess I figured I had to if I didn't want my whole creeping self to look like my face. Anyway, Sam, remember I told you I'd be around to see if you were all right. I just got here a little sooner than I planned."

"I'm glad about that too," said Amelia. "But Rosie, you don't have to call me 'Sam' anymore, you know."

"I know," Rosie said sheepishly. "I guess I just like calling you that. Is it all right?"

Amelia thought a moment and then smiled. "I guess I like it too," she concluded, thus winning a wide grin from Rosie. "But, Rosie, what are you doing with the broom and mop?"

"I'm sweeping and mopping, that's what," replied Rosie. "Appears that they're glad to have me too, especially since I said all I required was food and a roof over my head for the honor."

"Oh, *Rosie!*" said Amelia in dismay.

"Now, don't go 'oh Rosie-ing' me," said Rosie sternly. "Sweeping and mopping is what you were doing at the Castle Theatre for no more than the same rewards. And happy to have the situation, if I remember rightly. Anyway, I'd better be getting on with my work. I could be let off, and I haven't been here twenty-four hours! But more especially, we oughtn't to be seen talking together. No one knows we know each other, and we'd better keep it that way for now."

Amelia nodded her agreement to this.

"But look here, Sam," Rosie said, "I heard Mr. Quinge say he's to be away from two to four this afternoon. Mrs. McGregor naps then, and Sarah's off to see her ma. We've got lots to talk about, so if you'll be here, I'll be back to see you then."

"I will be!" said Amelia fervently. "But do be careful, Rosie. Make certain Mr. Quinge isn't about."

"I'll be certain, all right!" replied Rosie. "Anyway, it's nice and handy having the servants' stairs end up right here at your room."

"Servants' stairs?" asked Amelia. "What servants' stairs?"

Rosie looked startled. "Ones I just came up," he said. "Ones right behind me. Didn't you know they were there?"

Amelia shook her head. "The door's always been closed. I thought it was just another room."

"Well, it's stairs all right," said Rosie. "Dark as pitch, though. Next time I'm going to bring my lantern. See you when that old clock says it's two, Sam. And I might even have a surprise for you!" He gave Amelia a mischievous look, but without another word put his broom and mop over his shoulder and marched down the hall with his pail clanking in his hand.

Bong! Bong! Two o'clock came at last. Amelia, who had been waiting impatiently in her room, ran to her doorway and fixed her eyes on the door leading from the servants' stairs. The clock had no sooner finished announcing the time than that door opened a few inches, and Rosie's head poked out.

"Sam, go sit on your chair and close your eyes," he commanded.

"Why?" asked Amelia, wondering if this had something to do with Rosie's locket again. Surely Rosie was not going to turn back into Primrose, was he?

"Just do as I say, please," said Rosie firmly.

Amelia decided to do as she was asked—no, *ordered*—to do. She meekly sat down in her chair and closed her eyes. A few moments later, she felt something warm and heavy and fur-covered placed gently on her lap.

"You may open your eyes now," Rosie said.

Amelia hardly needed to open her eyes to know what Rosie had brought. "Choppers!" she cried. "Oh, Rosie, how did you ever manage to get him here?"

"Brought him here in a paper sack," said Rosie, who was beaming from ear to ear as he watched Amelia cradling the big, black cat. Choppers, of course, was filling Amelia's small room with a loud purr.

"Will you be allowed to keep him?" Amelia asked.

Rosie grimaced. "Don't know if I should tell you this, but when I asked Mr. Quinge if they ever had rats, he allowed, sour as a pickle, that they had one or two. Now, only in the basement, Sam, so don't go looking all alarmed. Anyway, then I showed him Choppers, and said he was the best ratter in the city, and hardly needed more to eat than what he could catch. So here we both are!"

"But what did you tell him about you, Rosie?" asked Amelia.

"Not much," Rosie replied. "Just said I had no ma or pa and was tired of being walloped by my uncle, so I decided to go off on my own, and needed a situation. Soon as I said I'd work for food and a roof, I got hired, no questions. I tell you, Sam, I think your Cousin Basil's in bad straits. Just look at this house—all those pictures and furnishings missing—sold, no doubt. Radiators turned down to freezing, and house all dark with lights turned down to near nothing. And Sarah said Mrs. McGregor told her there used to be lots more servants. I think the basement man just got let off, which is what I now am, shoveling coal and all the rest."

"Rosie, when you were at the Castle Theatre, you had to sweep, but you were the London canary as well," Amelia said. "You ought not to be just sweeping and mopping and shoveling coal."

"Never fear," said Rosie. "I won't be doing it forever. Might even go back to the Castle one day. By then, maybe Smeech and Turk might just think about how canaries can fly away if they don't get treated properly."

"Might they come after you here?" asked Amelia anxiously.

"They don't know that I know where you are," replied Rosie. "And they'd never think I'd dare look in Smeech's green book, or be smart enough to check with the cabby they had, who happens to be around the theatre all the time, which is actually how . . . " Rosie stopped suddenly, and grinned. "Oh, you should have seen them when they came back after they delivered you here. They really got themselves outfoxed this time. Collection plate! I'm not making this up, Sam, but Smeech was truly going to go visit whatever church it was he told Mr. Quinge he belonged to, and . . . and . . . and . . . " Rosie had begun to chortle, and was chortling so hard he could just barely continue. "And steal the money from the collection plate that your Cousin Basil said he'd put in it!"

"He wasn't!" Amelia giggled.

"He was. He said so. Cross my heart and hope to die if he didn't!" gasped Rosie. "And . . . and . . . and Turk told him if he believed anyone was actually going to put anything in any collection plate in any church in the world for him to go pick up, he was a bigger idiot than he appeared for ever wearing that collar in the first place.

By the time Rosie had finished this report, he was dancing around the room clutching his stomach, helpless with laughter. Amelia was now laughing just as hard, but instead of clutching her stomach, was clutching the bewildered Choppers. He, however, chose to remain on her lap and risk being squeezed to death rather than give up Amelia's tender ministrations to his ears.

Rosie finally collapsed onto the side of the cot. "And there's something else," he said when he was able to catch his breath. "They were both mad as hornets when they began thinking how they hadn't got any money and lost you into the bargain. Seems they figured your singing might be getting better, so here they'd gone and given up a London canary that would never lose its sweet voice, and not a penny to show for the loss. You should have seen their f . . . f . . . faces!"

This last was ample cause for them both to dissolve in laughter again. Then there was further uncontrolled merriment when Rosie wondered at the condition of their faces when they discovered their prize rat catcher had, as they would think, "upped and run away." Oh, that was too humorous even to imagine! But at last, when they had finally quieted down, Amelia suddenly remembered something that made the smile rapidly disappear from her face.

"Oh, Rosie," she said, "if they were so angry, that must be why you have that dreadful bruise. It's really all my fault for ever coming to the Castle Theatre."

"Now see here," said Rosie, "don't you go getting thoughts like that. This would have happened one day no matter what, because it's been getting worse all the time. They don't seem to know that walloping doesn't do a bit of good toward keeping a London canary from turning into a London crow. So you're not to go thinking this is all your fault—not ever! At any rate, we'd better talk about what's going on here. You haven't yet said much about your Cousin Basil. And did you ever find out what happened to your Cousin Charlotte?"

Cousin Basil! Cousin Charlotte! It was difficult for Amelia even to think about them, much less speak about them.

Rosie looked at her uneasily. "What's the matter, Sam? You've gone pale as a ghost."

"Rosie, it's turned out just as I thought. Cousin Basil doesn't want me here!" said Amelia, a catch in her voice. "I've only seen him twice. The first time was when Mr. Smeech and Mr. Turk brought me here, and Cousin Basil barely looked at me. He never even looked at me when he answered a question I asked."

"Didn't he say he was glad to see you, or anything like that?" asked Rosie.

Amelia shook her head.

"Creepers!" said Rosie.

"After that," Amelia continued, "the only time I saw him was when he went out the front door with Mr. Quinge. They were carrying Cousin Basil's traveling bags. It was right after I came here, and I have not seen him again. Oh, Rosie, how can I live in a house with someone who hates me so much?"

Rosie could only look at her, wordless. For how could anyone answer such a question?

"What about your Cousin Charlotte?" he asked finally.

"That was the question I asked Cousin Basil," Amelia said. "He told me he had no idea what happened to her. Then he said I must forget about her. Rosie, I don't think . . . " Amelia hesitated, her voice dropping to a whisper.

"Don't think what?" Rosie asked. "Why are you looking like that, Amelia?"

"I don't think Cousin Charlotte was Cousin Charlotte at all!" Amelia burst out.

Rosie's eyes flew wide open. "What do you mean?"

"You'd know what I meant if you saw Cousin Basil," replied Amelia. "I think Cousin Charlotte was really Cousin Basil!"

Rosie's jaw fell open. For a few moments, all he could do was stare at Amelia. "Creeping creepers!" he gasped. "Is that what the hat and veil were all about—a disguise?"

"I think it was," replied Amelia.

"But why would he do that?" Rosie asked.

"I don't know," Amelia said. "But I know it wasn't proper for me to travel with a strange gentleman, even if it was my cousin. I expect Cousin Charlotte couldn't come to London, so he just came as Cousin Charlotte."

"Well, it's creeping odd all the same," Rosie said. "And where do you suppose your Cousin Charlotte is now? What if there never was a Cousin Charlotte? Or what if there was, but isn't any-more?"

Amelia started. "Whatever do you mean, Rosie?"

Rosie took time to study the toes of his shoes. "I don't know what I mean," he said carefully, giving the feeling that he knew quite well what he meant. "Anyway," he went on, "it seems like a lot of trouble to go to just so he could end up losing you at the docks. Unless, though I hate to say it, Sam, maybe that's why he did do it."

"But then why did he come for me when I'd been kidnapped?" Amelia asked.

Rosie looked startled. "I didn't know about that. How did you find that out?"

"He told Mr. Smeech and Mr. Turk when they brought me here. I was already gone when Cousin Basil arrived there. But why did he come at all? Why . . . " Amelia stopped suddenly.

"What is it?" Rosie asked. "What have you thought of now, Sam?"

"Oh, Rosie, it's all so puzzling and frightening," Amelia said. "I just remembered something I haven't told you yet. The morning after I came here, I looked out the window and saw Mr. Quinge talking to . . . to . . . oh, Rosie, it was to Mrs. Dobbins!"

Rosie's eyes popped. "Mrs. Dobbins? You mean the one who lured you away from the docks?"

"I'm certain it was the very one," said Amelia. "I could never forget her."

"Wheeooo!" Rosie whistled. "There's a creeping twist! Maybe Mr. Quinge is behind you being kidnapped, and your Cousin Basil's just been taken in. Maybe nothing's the way it looks. Maybe lots of things, Sam. But right now I do know one thing. Cousin Charlotte or no Cousin Charlotte, Mr. Quinge might try again, if he's the one and still dealing with Mrs. Dobbins. I'll see what I can find out, and report soon as I can. Meantime, Sam, be careful. Keep your eyes fixed behind you. Things are just too creepy around here for my liking!"

Be careful! Keep your eyes fixed behind you!

No matter how Amelia twisted and turned those warnings in her head, they always came out the same way. Rosie was right, and it was what she would have to do.

Chapter XVIII

A Dangerous Exploration

Tap! Tap! Tap!

Amelia had no sooner stopped tossing and turning and begun to drift off into a fitful sleep, when the tapping caused her eyes to fly open.

Tap! Tap! Tap!

The sound came again, and now Amelia lost no time in climbing from her cot and throwing on her dress. After thinking over all the things she and Rosie had talked about, her stomach had been in a knot, and she had only picked at her supper. This must be kindhearted Sarah bringing what had been left on the plate.

"Who is it?" she whispered at the door, fully expecting to hear Sarah's low voice.

But the voice that replied did not belong to Sarah. "It's Rosie!"

Amelia swiftly threw open the door. Rosie was standing in the hall with a small oil lantern in his hand. It gave out only a dim, fluttering light, but it was enough for Amelia to see that Rosie's face was flushed, and his eyes bright with excitement as he slipped into the room.

"I've got something to tell you, Sam, but you'd better close the door. Mr. Quinge's light is out in his room, but roaches come out at night, and I don't know but what he's still crawling around the house."

Amelia promptly did as asked, for she had no more wish to see Mr. Quinge than Rosie did. "Did you find something out?" she asked eagerly.

"Well, it's only a guess," Rosie said, setting the lantern on the chest of drawers. "But I think it's a good one. You see, I finally began to think about how at all mealtimes I've been here, Mrs. McGregor fixes up a tray in the kitchen. Then when Sarah takes your dish to you in the dining room, and I'm busy eating my meal at the kitchen table, Mr. Quinge takes the tray away someplace. I just thought he was taking it to his room off the pantry, because he wouldn't want to be eating with the likes of me or Sarah or Mrs. McGregor. Tonight, when I got up to fetch a cup of milk from the icebox, I saw him carry the tray right past his room and on into the hall. Mrs. McGregor being busy at the sink, I ran to the hall and peeked in. There went Mr. Quinge right up the stairs with the tray! I didn't dare follow him, so I just ran back to the kitchen."

"Where do you suppose he takes it?" asked Amelia.

"As I said," replied Rosie, "all I have are guesses. I did ask Sarah about it, but her eyes just got big and scared, and she said I must only go about my business and not ask questions. All of which led to me thinking further. And the first thing I thought about, for no reason I know, was that turret at the front of the house."

Rosie paused to give Amelia a rueful grin. "Maybe because it was the first thing I saw when I came here, and I remembered thinking about how I'd escaped from one creeping castle only to end up at another! Anyway, the more I thought about it, the more I began to think that maybe your Cousin Basil never went away. Maybe he's . . . he's like a . . . a hermit, and doesn't like to talk to anyone or see anyone. Which might explain how he acts toward you, Sam. At any rate, I was thinking that maybe he sneaked back in, and that's where he's living, in a room under the turret, so he can creep up there and not have to see you or anybody he doesn't care to see."

"Do you *really* think that, Rosie?" asked Amelia.

Rosie shrugged. "Well, I do and I don't, because I do have a second guess. It's that somebody's being stored up there, maybe somebody that isn't quite right in the head, somebody your Cousin Basil wants you to forget about."

Amelia felt her heart begin to thump in her chest. "Do you mean you think it might be C . . . C . . . Cousin Charlotte?"

"Exactly!" said Rosie.

"Stored in the turret!" cried Amelia in horror.

"Happens in families all the time, I've heard," said Rosie matter-of-factly. "Anyway, how would you like to go exploring?"

"N . . . n . . . now?" stammered Amelia. "What . . . what about Mr. Quinge?"

"We'll be careful," Rosie said. "All we'll do is just go straight down the hall to where the turret is. We'll only see if we hear anything, and then we'll come right back. I'll go by myself anyway, but I'd like it if you'd go with me."

Amelia did not need to be asked again. She ran to the door and softly opened it. Rosie instantly picked up his lantern, turning the flame down so low it could hardly be called light at all. Then, silently, they started off down the hall.

Always so hushed and filled with shadows, it seemed to Amelia she would never get used to the hall. Now it was plunged into total darkness, all gaslights having been turned off for the night. They could have been traveling a tunnel in the middle of the earth. How small and helpless their tiny flame seemed! But they encountered no rats, no roaches, and no Mr. Quinge, and safely arrived at the end of the dark hall. Handing Amelia the lantern, Rosie put a finger to his lips and his ear to the door that appeared to be the one leading to the turret. Then he looked back at her with wide eyes.

"I think I can hear sounds," he whispered. "There must be someone in there!"

But the words had no sooner been said, than he snatched the lantern from Amelia's hand and swiftly turned off the flame. At that very moment, Amelia saw what Rosie had already seen, a faint light just beginning to make its way up the staircase.

"Quick!" he whispered. Grabbing Amelia's hand, he pulled her behind the heavy velvet draperies covering the window at the very end of the hall. Peering through the wire-thin opening where the draperies came together, they saw the light come closer and closer. Before it had even reached the door where they had been standing a moment earlier, they could see the flame from the lamp light up the sharp, sallow, hatchet face of—Mr. Quinge!

Barely breathing, hardly daring even to blink, they watched as he reached out a hand and tried the handle of the door. Twist. Twist. Twist. But the door stayed closed, for it was securely locked. With a satisfied half smile on his thin lips, Mr. Quinge turned on his heels and walked soundlessly down the hall back toward the stairwell. Then the light disappeared, and the hall was once again wrapped in darkness.

Now, with Rosie's lantern out, and no way to light it, they must make their way down the hall back to Amelia's room. Still, who would have dared to light the lantern anyway with Mr. Quinge awake and crawling about the house?

"I'm truly sorry, Sam," Rosie said as soon as they were safely back. "I shouldn't have asked you to do that."

"I wanted to go too, Rosie, or I wouldn't have," Amelia said at once.

"Truthfully?" asked Rosie.

"Truthfully!" replied Amelia. "And if we hadn't gone, we wouldn't have found out what we found out. There *is* someone in the turret room. You were right."

"The question is who and why," said Rosie, his brow wrinkled. "And what has Mr. Quinge to do with it all?"

"And how will we ever find out?" asked Amelia.

"Well, to start with," Rosie said, "I'm going to see if I can win Sarah over. It won't be easy. I think she's afraid of her own shadow, not to mention all the other creeping shadows in this house."

"I think it's more that she's afraid to lose her situation, Rosie," Amelia said. "She told me her mama's all alone with three young ones to care for. It would be dreadful if Sarah were to be let go and could no longer help."

Rosie's eyes filled with pity. "I didn't know that. But don't you worry. I'll be as careful as I can be. And whether I have anything to report, or whether I don't, I'll be back to see you tomorrow, most likely about the same time. And never you fear, even if not from Sarah, we'll find out what's going on around here. You can count on it!"

And Amelia believed that she could, for had Rosie not kept every promise he had made to her?

The next day was like every other one Amelia had spent at Cousin Basil's house—endlessly long and deadly dull. She wandered from her room down the wide, curving staircase, but soon crept right back up again, for what was there to interest her in that gloomy hall or parlor? Back in her room, she tried to bury herself in a lady's fashion magazine found in her chest of drawers, but soon grew restless and wandered back downstairs again. It seemed as if it would be forever before she would see Rosie again. At last, however, the long day ended.

As she finished her supper that night, drinking the last of her cup of milk alone in the cavernous dining room, she determined that she would stay up until he arrived. Trying to finish the tedious story in the fashion magazine, a sorrowful love story intended for grown-up ladies, would surely keep her wide awake.

But in her room, even though she was seated on her hard, uncomfortable little wood chair, the story did not seem to do a very good job of helping her eyes stay open. She could not remember when her eyelids had ever felt so heavy. But what was worse, her head had begun to ache terribly. Finally, she felt she could no longer hold open her eyes or hold up her drooping head. Perhaps, she thought, she should lie down on her cot for just a few minutes. She stood up, but she never did make it to her cot, for her legs gave out from under her and she crumpled to the floor. Then darkness rolled over her, and she knew no more.

When Amelia awoke the next morning, her head still ached dully, but she was now lying on her cot. She could not remember climbing into it, but climb into it she must have. Had she slept right through the night? Oh, no! What about Rosie? Had he come and tapped on her door, only to leave because there was no answer? Might he even have peeked in and seen her so dead asleep he did not want to awaken her? Oh, how could she have allowed herself to drop off to sleep like that when she had wanted so much to see him?

Then Amelia had a frightening thought. What if Rosie had not come at all because he had been caught by Mr. Quinge? How would she know? What person would she dare to ask?

Then as she lay on the cot, her head still aching and her arms and legs feeling strangely heavy, asking herself these questions, she suddenly noticed something curious about her window. Were her eyes playing tricks on her, or had it somehow shrunk to a tiny slice high up in the wall? And why was she hearing the clop-clop of horses' hooves and the sound of a baby crying?

Amelia allowed her eyes to drift slowly around the room, and then her blood turned to ice, for she saw that she was no longer in the room where she had slept the night before. She was back in the cellar room—the very same cellar room from which she had once escaped!

Chapter XIX

Oh, Could It Really Be?

Amelia was not only in the same prison, but still had on her same ugly dress. It was as if it were planned all along that she would be back in that dread place because, except for the sweater from Sarah, no one had provided her with a single new garment. The same ugly coat had been thrown over her to serve as a coverlet, for the cot had been stripped of all its bedding and had on it only the bare horsehair mattress and hard, lumpy pillow. Amelia was even still in her shoes, as if she had simply been dumped on the cot like a sack of potatoes.

Numb with fright and despair, but beyond tears, she lay for awhile staring at the ceiling. Oh, if only her head would stop aching! If only her arms and legs would not feel as if they were weighted down with lead! At last, she slowly dropped one leg over the side of the cot, then the other, and dragged herself to the doorway. The door was wide open, but not a sound came from beyond it. Holding the door frame to steady herself, Amelia peered out.

Although the furnishings were just as she remembered them, the room was otherwise deserted. Nor did it seem that it had just recently been deserted, for dust had begun to blanket everything. Over it all hung the smell of mold and mildew. The only sign, beyond Amelia herself, that anything human had entered the cellar was a lonely loaf of bread sitting on the table. It was clear from this that she was at least to be kept alive. But for what purpose? And for how long? Who, oh who, was doing this to her? And—why?

No one came to the cellar door—no one. There was nothing for Amelia to do but watch the pairs of feet marching relentlessly past the front window. She trembled lest one of them might pause and come stumping down the stairs to the cellar, yet she felt terrified at the thought that one of them might never stop. And then all at once, a key grated in the lock. Who was it to be? The horrible Mrs. Shrike? The thieving Mrs. Dobbins? Who? The key turned in the lock. The door opened. And a head poked in.

"Sam? Sam? Are you here? It's me, Rosie!"

"Rosie!" cried Amelia.

Yes, it truly was Rosie stepping through the doorway into the cellar! His eyes darted nervously around the room.

"Whew!" he breathed. "No one here but you. And am I glad *you're* still here! I had a scare when I first looked in and didn't see you. Creepers! I thought you were already gone. Come on, quick, get your coat. We've got to get out of here!"

Seeing the state Rosie was in, Amelia did not stop to ask questions but ran for her coat. "Where . . . where are we going?" she asked as she scurried back.

"I'll tell you," Rosie replied. "But first, Sam, before we go through that door, I have to tell you you're going to see someone who's going to frighten you at first. But you mustn't be frightened. It's all right, I promise you. And I'll explain all about it, as soon as we're on our way."

Taking Amelia by the hand, Rosie pulled her along with him as he raced out the door and up the steps. And there, standing in front of a waiting cab was—oh, no, how could it be? But it was.

For how could Amelia ever forget the big, burly man, seen only once but never forgotten, whose name was—Elmo Dobbins!

"Oh, no!" Amelia cried, pulling back. "Rosie, *no!*"

"Sam, you have to believe me," Rosie said sternly. "It's really and truly all right. Elmo came along in case there was any creeping trouble, and I was powerfully happy to have him and his fists, if needed, to rescue you."

As if the latter point needed to be proved, Elmo Dobbins doubled up his fists and gave Amelia an enormous smile. "That's right, miss," he said cheerfully.

"Anyway," Rosie said, exchanging a significant glance with Elmo Dobbins, "Elmo's got an errand to run, so he won't be coming with us."

"But you never have told me where we're going," Amelia complained.

"I'll tell you that once I've explained everything else," said Rosie.

Amelia had to be satisfied with that until they had climbed into the cab. Rosie had waved to the still-smiling Elmo Dobbins, and they were bowling down the street.

"Oh!" Amelia suddenly gasped.

"What is it?" asked Rosie.

"I just remembered I never asked how you found me!" exclaimed Amelia.

"You haven't had the time," said Rosie matter-of-factly. "But it so happens *that* is exactly what I had in mind to explain to you. And this is how it all came about, Sam.

"When I came to see you last night, I heard voices just outside the door from the stairs, so I quickly turned off my lantern and cracked open the door. I couldn't see anything, but I could hear everything, because whoever was there was thinking they were the only ones around. It was two men. I don't remember their exact words, but they went something like this.

" 'Out like a light. You shouldn't have any trouble,' one of them said. I knew the voice. It belonged to Mr. Quinge!

" 'Still don't see why you couldn't have worked it the other way,' number two man grumbled. That one was a voice I didn't know, Sam.

" 'Because, as I've told you a dozen times, Bert,' Mr. Quinge said, 'Mrs. Dobbins could not have been duped into doing it again. She was already getting suspicious about it, and came around to talk to her old friend Mrs. McGregor and to Sarah. I managed to keep her away from them, but there isn't any way she'd do it again, or anything like it.'

" 'When are they coming for the girl?' asked number two man.

" 'The SS *Sharker* docked this morning and leaves tomorrow afternoon.' Mr. Quinge replied. 'Pymm has it all set up so they'll come for her sometime before then. Good thing she showed up here so we're able to get her back there in time.'

" 'Is that Mrs. Shrike you hired last time going to be there with her?' asked number two man.

" 'No need,' replied Mr. Quinge. 'She won't be there long enough.'

" 'You're not expecting me to wait there for them, are you?' snarled number two man.

" 'No! No! No!' snapped Mr. Quinge sweetly. 'You just see she's safely locked up. Mrs. Dobbins still has the key we gave her, worse luck, but by the time she learns about this, the girl will be gone.'

" 'Beats me why anyone wants a girl with her hair all chopped off and dressed like a rag bag,' then said number two man.

" 'Never mind what beats you,' replied Mr. Quinge. 'Quality shows through, and quality like this will fetch a top price as somebody's second or third wife, where she's going, Pymm says. Anyway, we had to get her looking like this in case somebody got nosey and suspicious. She'll be fixed up before she gets where she's going. Here, take her coat, will you, and put it over her. We don't want her arriving in a sickly condition. Now, get going!'

"So that was the whole conversation close as I can remember, Sam," Rosie said. "Anyhow, soon as it was light, I went and woke Sarah. I remembered what you told me about her, but I also knew you were in grave danger. She agreed with me, and told me never mind about asking questions, she'd tell me anything I needed to know. So I told her I had to find Mrs. Dobbins to learn where you'd been taken, and borrow the key to get in. Sarah went without a quiver to learn Mrs. Dobbins's whereabouts from Mrs. McGregor, and even gave me money from what she's been saving, because she said I needed a cab to get there. But don't you worry, Sam. I'll see she gets it back. At any rate, that's the whole story of how I got to where you were."

"Oh, Rosie!" cried Amelia, too overcome to say more. But it must have been clear to Rosie from the tone of her voice and the way in which she looked at him that she knew he had saved her from the most terrible of fates. And, oh, how much his brave efforts were appreciated!

"So now about where we're going," he said quickly, wanting, it appeared, to take all interest off himself. "Well, we're going to someone who can't wait, she says, to make certain the dear child, which is you, Sam, is safe and well. She never did know you were at the house, because Sarah and Mrs. McGregor were threatened by Mr. Quinge not to tell her. I suspect you've guessed by now that the person is your friend—Mrs. Dobbins!"

"Oh, my dear child, I can't believe you really are here before me, safe and sound," Mrs. Dobbins kept saying over and over again as she sat with Amelia and Rosie in her tiny parlor.

"And how," she said, "could I have been so foolish and taken in? What a stupid old thing I've become! Imagine being persuaded to invite you to that dreadful place because, as I was told, your life was in danger, and all depended on your being hidden there secretly for awhile. And think of allowing myself to believe those ugly clothes were intended to keep you safely disguised. Can you ever forgive me child? Indeed you must, or it will break my heart, indeed it will!" Tears once again flowed down her worn, kindly face as they had been doing from the very moment Amelia stepped through the door.

How much easier it was to accept that this little woman with the rosy cheeks and soft eyes was what she had appeared to be at the very beginning than ever to believe that she was a—a thief and a—a kidnapper! And of course Amelia forgave Mrs. Dobbins—no, now Nanny Dobbins again—and said so over and over.

The minutes became hours, and all flew by, with Mrs. Dobbins being forgiven wholeheartedly again and again. It seemed she would never tire of hearing how Amelia had escaped from Mrs. Shrike, whom Mrs. Dobbins had never even heard of, and how Amelia had found Rosie, now become a hero in the sight of the two other pairs of eyes present, greatly to his embarrassment.

But curiously, all the while this cozy conversation was taking place, Mrs. Dobbins would run to the window from time to time and peer anxiously out. At length, the sound of horses' hooves was heard, and a carriage stopped at her door.

"Thank heavens, Elmo has done his job!" she said. Then she came to sit beside Amelia on the tiny settee and took both of Amelia's hands in her own.

"Dear child," she said, "you must be prepared for a very great shock and surprise. I hope it will not alarm you, indeed I do!" Then she gently pulled Amelia from the settee and led her to the front door just as the bell was heard to ring.

Mrs. Dobbins quickly opened the door to reveal two people standing there. For barely more than a heartbeat, they stared at Amelia and she stared at them. Then, with a cry, Amelia ran toward them, and it did not seem to matter that she could not choose which arms to run into, for both pairs enfolded her. And Amelia found that she was no longer beyond tears, for they flowed down her cheeks, mingling with the tears of those who held her. They were Aunt Felicia and—and Papa! Yes, it was John Fairwick, Amelia's very own papa, alive and standing there before her!

Chapter XX

Wicked! Wicked!

John Fairwick, not lost in the terrible hotel fire after all, but only falsely imprisoned! John Fairwick, weakened and wan, but still alive! The explanation for how this had happened could wait until later, however, when all would be told, all revealed.

For the moment, hearts and minds were filled only with the joys of being together again, of trying to believe that this miraculous event was really happening, and wondering if any of them would ever believe it. But while Amelia was being hugged and kissed, and then hugged again, there were some things it seemed impossible not to speak of and marvel at. For was it not wonderful and serendipitous that Amelia and Rosie—then Primrose—had become shipboard friends, so that Amelia had a friend to go to when she escaped her cellar prison? Yet how dangerous that journey had been! The telling of it could, of course, only inspire further hugs and kisses of thankfulness that no harm had come to her.

But how could enough ever be said about Rosie? For what if he had not come to Cousin Basil's house in the first place? What might have become of Amelia? It was too terrible to contemplate, and how wonderful that now no one needed to.

Indeed, with so much to be happy about, little was said about Amelia's curious appearance—her dress that made her look no better than a street urchin, or her cropped head. Who would have had the heart to say much, with poor little Mrs. Dobbins wringing her hands over the part she had played in providing the ugly garment, or Rosie wishing he had not been so clumsy when trimming Amelia's hair? If Aunt Felicia shed a tear from time to time over it, the tear was quickly wiped away.

Aunt Felicia? No, Aunt Felicia no longer! For of all things, one of the most joyous was that John Fairwick and Felicia Charlton had been married by the captain aboard the ship crossing the ocean, and Aunt Felicia had now become Felicia Fairwick— Amelia's new mama!

Oh, what happiness there was filling that small room! How wonderful if it could go on forever. But it could not. And though it seemed no time at all had passed, John Fairwick at last stood up and said, "Now, there is a cousin we must visit. And there are people waiting there for us, I believe."

That was the signal that they were all to return to Cousin Basil's house. How different for Amelia to be going there with Mama and Papa, accompanied by Mrs. Dobbins and Rosie! How different from arriving in the custody of Mr. Smeech and Mr. Turk! Still, Amelia did not look forward to a return to that grim and gloomy house.

For all the cheerfulness, smiles, and laughter so recently enjoyed, the journey to Cousin Basil's house was remarkably somber and quiet. In the cab, Amelia sat between Papa and her new mama, one hand being held and squeezed frequently by each. Across from them sat Mrs. Dobbins and Rosie. The latter, Amelia noted, seemed to be sunk in deep and gloomy silence.

As she thought about it, it came to her that he had become very quiet, and not at all his usual cheery self, before they had even left

Mrs. Dobbins' house. But perhaps it was small wonder. For here was Amelia gloriously happy with the amazing return of Papa, and now with a new and beloved mama, and what had Rosie to look forward to? Was he to return to Cousin Basil's house and continue mopping and sweeping and carrying buckets of coal? Or was he to return to the Castle Theatre and face being "walloped" on a regular basis by Mr. Smeech? All this was too terrible to contemplate. Amelia would have to speak to Papa about it. Something must be done!

Another cab was already stopped in the driveway when they arrived. Before they all started for the door, John Fairwick restrained them for a moment while he went to talk to someone inside that cab.

"All appears to be in order," he said, returning with a look of satisfaction on his face. "Shall we go in?"

Rosie immediately started away down the path toward the back of the house.

"Where are you going, young man?" John Fairwick asked at once.

"To . . . to the servants' entrance," stammered Rosie.

"You'll do no such thing," said John Fairwick. "You'll come along with us."

Rosie, recognizing the voice of authority, meekly turned around and when the rest of the party entered the house, he entered with them.

The door, of course, was opened by Mr. Quinge. It would have been difficult to describe the expression on his face when he saw those assembled on the doorstep, one of them being Amelia, whom the very night before he had seen carried senseless from the house. It would be safe to say that all color drained from his sallow face. It might also be safe to say that his sharp eyes had taken in the presence of the black coach in the driveway, and recognized its meaning, that any thoughts of escaping the house were not to be considered.

"Good afternoon," said John Fairwick pleasantly. "I should like to see Mr. Desmond, please."

"I'm sorry, sir," replied Mr. Quinge, "but Mr. Desmond is not in at the moment."

"Well, in that case," said John Fairwick smoothly, "we should like to come in and wait for him."

Mr. Quinge hesitated the barest fraction of a second. "I don't believe I can permit that, sir."

"Oh, I think Mr. Desmond would be very disappointed to return and learn that we had not been allowed in," said John Fairwick in no less pleasant a voice than when he had first spoken. "You see, I am John Fairwick, just arrived from London, here with Mrs. Fairwick. We have never met face-to-face, but I do believe Mr. Desmond is acquainted with my daughter, Amelia, who has her young friend with her, and Mr. Desmond's former nanny, Mrs. Dobbins."

John Fairwick and the gentlemen waiting in the black coach in the driveway really had had no idea of whether Basil Desmond was at home or away and, if away, when he would return. By now, however, it was known through Mrs. Dobbins, who had it from her good friend Mrs. McGregor, that he was expected to return that afternoon. So John Fairwick was quite secure in stating that he would await Cousin Basil's arrival. And how could Mr. Quinge inform a recently arrived relative, however distant, that he would not be allowed in the house?

"In which case then," he said, his face frozen, "please do enter."

He ushered them all into the parlor, Rosie included. For how, likewise, could Mr. Quinge inform a young relative of Mr. Desmond that her friend must retire to the kitchen?

The one person who did not enter the parlor was Mrs. Dobbins, who remained behind in the hall. As the others found seats in the cold, forbidding parlor, they could hear words being exchanged in the hall that were not entirely of a friendly nature.

What could be the cause of the argument, for argument it clearly was? When it ended, however, Mrs. Dobbins still did not enter the parlor. Where had she gone? And why?

In the meantime, the minutes dragged slowly by. The dismal parlor caused hushed conversation between Amelia, Papa, and Mama almost to fade away entirely. Rosie, still sunk in silence, spoke only when spoken to.

Bong! Bong! Bong!

The great clock struck the hour of three in the afternoon, and almost at the same time, the rustle of silk was heard in the hall. Through the door into the parlor, hand in hand with a beaming, misty-eyed Mrs. Dobbins, walked—no, *floated* on silken skirts—a young woman. In some eyes she might well have been called beautiful, but she was unquestionably extraordinarily handsome. Her thick auburn hair was drawn up at the back of her head into a gleaming cascade of curls, arranged to fall becomingly over one shoulder. She wore an elegant, yet unadorned, silk dress of an amethyst color that served to heighten the color of her remarkable lavender-blue eyes, and perfectly complement the high, rose-pink color of her flushed cheeks.

"I am Cousin Charlotte," she said simply.

Cousin Charlotte? Was this the Cousin Charlotte who had brought Amelia from London, only to desert her on the docks of New York City? Oh, no! This beautiful woman could never have been that Cousin Charlotte. *She* had been, just as Amelia had guessed, Cousin Basil in disguise. But why could *this* lovely woman not have been sent for Amelia? Why had she needed to be locked up in the turret? Surely, oh surely, it could not have been because she was—was deranged, as Rosie had suggested. Why then?

But John Fairwick and Rosie had no sooner jumped to their feet than Mr. Quinge was seen rushing to open the front door. It was Cousin Basil returning to his house. All eyes were on him as he carefully peeled off his gloves, then handed them with his coat and hat to Mr. Quinge. Mr. Quinge leaned over slightly to whisper something to him. After a moment of thought, Cousin Basil shrugged and entered the parlor.

"Good afternoon, Charlotte," he said, "how nice to have you join us. I understand from Mr. Quinge that we have visitors." His face was deadly pale, and he appeared to have a slight twitch at one corner of his thin lips. Otherwise, no one could have imagined that his guests might be the last persons in the world he wanted to see, or that he had been holding his sister a prisoner in his house.

"Mr. Quinge tells me that you are John Fairwick," Cousin Basil continued. "How nice that we finally meet each other after all these years."

The two men shook hands, but it was a handshake hardly noted for any warmth of feeling.

"And this is . . . ?" said Cousin Basil, turning to Amelia's new mama.

"My wife, Felicia," said John Fairwick. "And you, of course, know my daughter, Amelia, here with her young friend."

"Of course," said Cousin Basil, the corners of his lips twitching a trifle more noticeably. Then he turned to his sister. "Won't you be seated, Charlotte, so John and I may also make ourselves comfortable?"

"Thank you, Basil, but I prefer to remain as I am," Cousin Charlotte replied, her voice cold and distant.

"Perhaps, Basil, there is no need for us to, as you say, make ourselves comfortable," John Fairwick said. "I believe you must know why I am here?"

Cousin Basil, with studied deliberation, flicked an imaginary speck of dust from his cuff. "I believe I do," he said. "I don't suppose, however, that you would care to tell me how I was found out?"

"Oh, suspicion on the part of my solicitor, a consultation with members of Scotland Yard, followed by a trip to the country in question and some very clever investigative work. All of which led to the clerk in the office of my overseas business connection who was providing information to his brother, your accomplice, Mr. Pymm. But that hardly matters now, does it?" John Fairwick said. "I do wonder, however, why you simply did not have me murdered in jail after conspiring to have me falsely accused of thievery on the streets and arrested."

"I confess that you might have been murdered," Cousin Basil replied coolly. "What saved you from that fate was your hotel burning to the ground, with you presumably in it. We believed that would keep anyone from conducting the investigation, which would most certainly have taken place had you merely disappeared. It happened anyway, regrettably. Pymm did assure me that prisoners in that country were easily hidden from the world, so you would languish there until you perished. He still, however, did recommend the other alternative. I suppose I should have listened to him."

"And why didn't you?" asked John Fairwick.

Cousin Basil shrugged. "I didn't want blood on my hands, if it wasn't necessary. Pymm knew that."

"Well, it seems you had some equally despicable plans for my precious daughter, and we have your sister Charlotte to thank for managing to get a cable to Felicia, begging her to come here as quickly as possible."

"How clever of you, Charlotte," Cousin Basil said, his lips curled into a cynical smile. "How on earth *did* you manage that?"

"Oh, I managed all right!" cried Cousin Charlotte. "After all, don't forget that your Mr. Quinge was not the only one waiting on me, and I was able to persuade that poor, frightened child, Sarah, to fetch me paper and pen, and then take my cable away from this house to be sent. I even advised Felicia Charlton that her response was to come to the home of Mrs. Dobbins, lest it fall into your hands. You weren't so clever after all, Basil. Clever! What a strange word to apply to you—you who ruined your life with gambling. Look at this house! Half of everything gone to pay your debts. And when you concluded that the house itself would go, you went to desperate and horrible measures to acquire the family fortune you always thought should be yours."

"Are you quite finished, Charlotte?" Cousin Basil said, his lips now twitching almost uncontrollably. "Shouldn't you go back upstairs and rest?"

"I think Charlotte should be allowed to finish," interrupted John Fairwick. "I believe we should all like to hear what she has to say."

Cousin Basil did not even turn to John Fairwick, but remained silent, and continued to stare at his sister. She stared back at him, her eyes flashing.

"I'm certain you know, Basil, that I had no suspicion of your hand in arranging for the death of your cousin's husband. So how could I possibly imagine that you would attempt to rid yourself of his child, even knowing that she had inherited her mother's fortune, so long coveted by you, and would, upon her father's death, inherit his wealth as well? Even when I was tricked into leaving her alone at the docks, and taken from there at knifepoint, I did not at first, in my innocence and fright, connect my abduction with John Fairwick's child.

"But when I was brought here, and my fear for myself had subsided, I realized, to my horror, that you might have something in mind for that child. It did not take much imagination to know why. The question was, what was to be her fate at your hands? And then I made a discovery in the turret that revealed to me what you, my once revered brother, were capable of doing, and I knew the child was in grave danger. So I sent the cable to Felicia Charlton, begging her to waste no time in coming here and only praying that it was not too late."

Cousin Basil had not been disguised as Cousin Charlotte after all! Cousin Charlotte, who had brought Amelia from London, was the exact same Cousin Charlotte who now stood in this very room! But how was it possible that that cold, unfeeling, frightening woman with the grim, veiled black hat could be connected in any way to this handsome, warm person now before them? What could possibly be the explanation?

"Gambling!" cried Cousin Charlotte. "Oh, to what lengths it has led you, Basil! What degradation! What ruination!"

At this, Mrs. Dobbins's lips were seen to tighten sternly. "Wicked! Wicked!" she burst out. "You were always a wicked, naughty boy, Basil. Tormenting your sister. Teasing the animals. Playing tricks on your Nanny Dobbins. But who was to know you would play such a trick on her, making her believe she was helping keep this child from danger, when all along it was only to help you with your wicked plans. Oh, who was to know you would come to such an end? Who was to know!" Overcome, Mrs. Dobbins threw her face into her hands.

"Yes, who was to know, indeed," said Cousin Charlotte. "And who was to know you would continue to torment me when we grew up? You would not forgive my interest in the theatre, and would forgive even less my marriage to an actor. As if gambling were somehow a more honorable profession! And after persuading me that I should leave the country with my husband because I was a disgrace to our family name, you then persuaded him to leave before me, bribed him to do so, as you later informed me, even as I lay in my bed, my mind gone mad by the loss of our infant. Of course, I never heard from my husband again."

Cousin Charlotte paused to look sadly at Amelia before continuing.

"And this poor, poor child was to end up suffering for it. Believing that I had been betrayed by my husband, having learned to hate the theatre and all connected with it, and having lost my child, I turned hard and cold. I vowed to have nothing further to do with the theatre, nor ever give my heart to anyone, especially any child. But I did connect to the theatre for one final act, using theatrical wiles to hide myself behind a mask that made me that hideous person who came to fetch Amelia. Oh, how it has broken my heart to remember the look on her face, a poor motherless child who had only just lost her father. I only hope that someday I may be forgiven!"

"Surely you have now said everything you need to say, Charlotte," snapped Cousin Basil.

Cousin Charlotte threw her head up. "Oh no, not quite," she said, her voice breaking. "You see, Basil, I found the letters! Those letters showed me to what depths your treachery could take you, perhaps even so low as the murder of a child! Realizing that is why I made the desperate attempt to reach someone who could save Amelia Fairwick from such a fate.

"Had you forgotten you had those letters hidden away in the secret hiding place you and I had in the turret when we were children? Those letters, Basil, all from my wonderful, dear husband Edward Blakiston, who waited and waited for a letter from me, but never received one because I never received his. And there was even the letter from that kind woman letting me know that he had contracted a terrible illness, and was no more.

"But it was from Edward's letters that I learned the truth of what really happened so many years ago. The truth, Basil! For you had never bribed him, as you so cleverly put it, but had merely given him the means to set up a home to receive and be ready for me when I should have recovered from my madness. But I learned something far worse than that. It was that the child, *our* child, the infant you told me I had lost—and so caused me to go mad from grief—was with him. Thus you had been assured that, with my life destroyed, I would remain in this house as your devoted sister and housekeeper. That day is past, and my child might still be alive. I intend to go and find out what happened to it, if the search takes me to my dying breath."

Cousin Basil gave a careless shrug. "Well, if you must, you must." With a weary sigh, he turned to John Fairwick. "There seems to be no purpose served in my remaining here. Would you like to escort me to the gentlemen in the waiting coach? I ask that at least you spare me the embarrassment of having them come for me and leading me from my own house in handcuffs. I suppose Quinge and Pymm will be wanted as well?"

"Oh yes," said John Fairwick. "Mr. Quinge may accompany you now. Mr. Pymm is, I believe, being apprehended even as we speak."

Cousin Basil started for the doorway, but then hesitated and turned again to his sister. "Well, my dear, I should at least like it noted that I always preferred something other than—murder."

"Basil, you are truly contemptible!" said Cousin Charlotte. "Consigning your cousin to rot in some prison hole in a barbaric country where he would never see the light of day again. And having his child doomed to a fate that for her would be far worse than death. What a coward you are and always were. You never could look at your victims, could you? Oh, what devious arrangements you made so you never had to see the child! And how I would love to have seen your face when she appeared on your doorstep!"

"I wish you could have too, if it would have brought you any pleasure, my dear," replied Cousin Basil. "Well, I wish you all a good day. Shall we go, John?"

A heavy pall of silence fell over the room as John Fairwick escorted Cousin Basil and Mr. Quinge to the waiting coach. Cousin Charlotte remained standing as she had when she came in, staring ahead, yet not appearing to be seeing anything. But as soon as John Fairwick came back to the parlor, Rosie, who had been as silent as the rest, suddenly started across the room with slow, hesitant steps. As he neared Cousin Charlotte, he pulled something from his pocket and held it out to her.

She looked at what lay in his hand, and picked it up. The object was the gold locket Rosie had shown Amelia in her cabin aboard the ship. Cousin Charlotte opened it, and all color drained from her face.

"Where did you get this?" she asked hoarsely.

"It . . . it belonged to . . . to my mother," said Rosie.

With a cry, Cousin Charlotte fell to the floor, senseless.

Chapter XXI

Cousins in the Castle

No sooner had Cousin Charlotte been restored, and color returned to her cheeks, than John Fairwick simply and gently as possible told of how the young boy, now known to be her lost son, had come to be in that very room. And was it any wonder that her eyes flooded with tears as the story unfolded? But when it had finally ended and all tears wiped away, what a different place the parlor became!

Mrs. Dobbins began to bustle around the room, throwing open the draperies and letting in the full, bright winter sunshine. And when it was remarked that wood lay in the desolate, long-unused fireplace, Rosie immediately busied himself with starting a fire. He seemed eager to have something with which to occupy himself, because, as could clearly be seen, he felt uncomfortable and shy at suddenly having found himself with a mama. She, in turn, seemed just as shy and uncomfortable about suddenly having *him*. Neither one appeared able to look at the other without quickly looking away.

In any event, a fire was soon snapping and crackling merrily in the fireplace. That, added to the sunlight streaming in the window, made the parlor the most cheerful of places.

"And high time, too, indeed it is," said Mrs. Dobbins, "that this house was returned to the way it used to be before that naughty Master Basil took to his gambling ways, if you'll excuse me for saying it, Miss Charlotte. But now it appears to me that all you poor dears might be in need of refreshment, so I shall excuse myself and go see Mrs. McGregor and Sarah about it, indeed I will. And won't they be astonished at . . . " Her voice faded away as she flew off, all atwitter, into the hall, hardly able to hide her delight at once again playing her role of Nanny Dobbins in charge!

With hearts and minds so full of all that had recently taken place, however, conversation flagged in the parlor while she was away. But as soon as she returned bearing a tray of cups and saucers and teapot, followed by Sarah with plates of biscuits and thinly sliced currant cake, the atmosphere in the parlor brightened.

Then, as Sarah held the cups for Mrs. Dobbins to pour tea, Rosie suddenly did something startling. He ran over and took one of the cups from Sarah, turned and, carefully balancing it, carried it across the room and handed it to Cousin Charlotte. Then, with one hand across his chest, the other flung into the air, he made a sweeping stage bow.

For a few moments, it seemed that no one in the parlor knew what to make of this. Then, smiling at each other, John and Felicia Fairwick began to applaud. A tiny smile appeared at the corners of Cousin Charlotte's mouth. Her lavender-blue eyes began to dance. Then all at once she threw back her head, laughing merrily.

"Do you know something, Edward?" she said, for that was his true name, being the same as that of his papa. "I believe that you and I are going to get on famously!"

Rosie's reply was a grin as wide as any he had ever produced in his life!

"My," said Mrs. Dobbins, clasping her hands together, her round face creased with pleasure, "how lovely it will be to have a child's voice ringing down these halls again!"

"Oh, Nanny Dobbins," said Cousin Charlotte with a sad smile, "you mustn't count on that, at least not from Edward and me. I'm afraid the house will have to be sold."

"Oh no!" cried Felicia Fairwick. "Not this wonderful old house! Hasn't it been in the Desmond family for a very long time?"

"For generations," replied Cousin Charlotte.

"Am I right," John Fairwick said, "in thinking that the house is owned outright, and unpaid back taxes are the reason it must be sold?"

"Yes," replied Cousin Charlotte simply. "As you can see, Basil has sold almost all the family heirlooms, but they were not enough to feed his gambling habits and keep the house as well. He grew desperate and then devised his fiendish plan. How grateful I am that it failed! The house must go, but I will see it go gladly, knowing what would have had to happen for my brother to keep it."

"When you say 'my brother,' do I take that to mean that he is the sole owner of the house?" asked John Fairwick.

"Being the son and heir, yes, of course," replied Cousin Charlotte. "He invited me to live with him when I was 'deserted' by my husband."

"Well, I don't feel the house should go to strangers. Nor need it be sold for taxes," John Fairwick said. He turned to Felicia Fairwick, who gave him an encouraging nod. "We owe you and Ros . . . that is to say, Edward, such a debt of gratitude there is almost no way to repay it. I have no idea what the taxes might be, but I'm certain that Felicia and I are well able to make them right. It surely seems the very least we can do. As for your brother's ownership of the house, it would seem to me that as the house will have to be sold for taxes in any event, there is no reason why I should not buy the house and have the title transferred to you as sole owner. I shall seek legal counsel on this, of course, but I certainly see no problem with it. Just let me have the deed, the tax bills, and . . . "

"Oh, John," Cousin Charlotte interrupted, her eyes filled with tears, "I cannot! I cannot! How can I let you . . . "

"My dear, you can! You will! And you must!" said John Fairwick. "But will you then be able to maintain the house? Because if you can't, we will also want to . . . "

"No! No! No more!" cried Cousin Charlotte. "I do still have my own income. Small though it may be, with proper management, we can live here. I might take in paying guests" —she looked at Rosie with twinkling eyes— "theatrical people, of course. Castle Desmond, we can call ourselves . . . Castle Desmond, a home for the arts. We can put on little performances here in this great room, and . . . oh yes, I think Edward and I will do very well here!"

"Then, we'll consider it settled," said John Fairwick. "I should like to take care of all the particulars before we sail for London. Of course, we will be back in a month or two, but . . . "

"Papa!" Amelia exclaimed. "Are we coming back?"

"I've always told you we would one day," John Fairwick replied. "Don't you want to?"

"I think I do now," Amelia replied. "But, Papa . . . " She leaned over to whisper something to him.

"I'm sure it's fine with your mama and me," he said. "But I do think you should ask your Cousin Charlotte."

Amelia trailed shyly to her cousin, posed her questions, and received a smiling nod. After which, Amelia then flew out to the kitchen to see Sarah. Amelia returned shortly with the happy news that Sarah would oh so much love to be employed by Amelia's papa and mama, and be Amelia's companion on a lovely sea voyage before settling in her new home with them. But for all this, however, Sarah herself must pay a price. And the price was that she must never again address Amelia as "miss," but always call her Amelia as her Polly had always done. It need hardly be mentioned that Sarah happily agreed to this!

"Now," said Cousin Charlotte as soon as Amelia had returned

to the parlor, "I would like to suggest that we excuse the children so they can go exploring this wonderful house. I have the feeling both of them would love to go up in the turret, and I challenge them to find the secret hiding place! Oh, and you might try looking in some of the other rooms to see if you can't find Amelia's steamer trunk and her portmanteau. They both must be someplace, and I'm certain her parents would like to see her out of that *costume* as soon as possible."

Rosie was on his feet in an instant. "Come on, Sam, let's go!"

"Sam?" John Fairwick turned to Felicia Fairwick with a puzzled frown. "Where on earth did that come from?"

"Oh, Papa!" said Amelia in a tone that suggested he really should not have had to ask. "That was my name when I had to be a boy at the Castle Theatre, and was learning to be another London canary."

"Oh, I see," said John Fairwick meekly, as he watched his daughter go flouncing out of the parlor.

"Do you suppose she'll let me be called Rosie instead of Edward?" Rosie whispered, stopping suddenly at the foot of the curved staircase.

"If you mean your mama," replied Amelia, "I expect she'll let you have anything you want."

"Well then, do you think she'll let me have a pony?" asked Rosie.

"I'm certain she'd want you to have one if you wanted it," said Amelia. "But you ought to remember that she won't have a great deal of money."

"That's right," said Rosie. "Oh well, I do have Choppers. I hope I'll be able to keep him."

"I expect you will," said Amelia.

They started to climb the stairs, and Rosie sighed. "I expect I'll be having to go to school as well."

"I expect you will," said Amelia, offering no hope on that score.

"But at least I won't be getting walloped anymore," Rosie said.

"Oh no!" said Amelia. "Oh *no*, Rosie!"

But when they reached the head of the stairs, Rosie came to another sudden stop. "Creeping creepers, Sam, I just thought of something!"

Amelia's heart leaped into her throat. Had Rosie come up with one of his tales offering some terrible explanation of what had happened, or was going to happen?

"Wh . . . wh . . . what?" she stammered.

"Well," said Rosie, "it just came to me that if my ma is your cousin, and she is, then doesn't that make us cousins as well?"

"Oh yes!" breathed Amelia happily. "It does!"

Rosie shook his head in wonder. "Think of it! First, I find out I have a ma. And then I find I have a cousin as well, which is you."

"And," added Amelia, "I have Papa back. And I have a new mama. And I find *I* have a new cousin, which is *you*."

"And do you remember when you thought I was a creeping princess, Sam?" Rosie said. "Well, here I am going to live in a . . . a creeping castle, or sort of one, anyway. You know something? This is better than any play that I ever heard about."

"Oh, it's more like a fairy tale!" said Amelia delightedly.

"So I suppose," Rosie said with a wide grin, "that we all have to live happily after!"

And who was there in the castle who would argue with that?

Wallace, Barbara
Wallace   Brooks,
        Cousins in the
        castle

15.00

12|17 2|19
   9   10
Celli4   10/18

WITHDRAWN

OCT 1997

Manhasset Public Library
Manhasset, New York 11030
Telephone: 627-2300

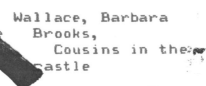